Killer in Drag

Killer in Drag

by Ed Wood, Jr.

Four Walls Eight Windows
New York /London

© 1999 Estate of Edward D. Wood, Jr.

Published in the United States by
Four Walls Eight Windows
39 West 14th Street, room 503
New York, NY 10011
http://www.fourwallseightwindows.com

U.K. offices:
Four Walls Eight Windows/Turnaround
Unit 3 Olympia Trading Estate
Coburg Road, Wood Green
London N22 6TZ

First edition published in 1965 by Star News Co. Four Walls Eight
Windows edition published in 1999.

Library of Congress Cataloguing-in-Publication Data:
Wood, Edward D. (Edward Davis), 1924-1978.
Killer in drag / by Edward D. Wood, Jr.
p. cm.
ISBN 1-56858-120-3
I.Title.
PS3573.05925K551999
813'.54--dc2198--49260
CIP

10 9 8 7 6 5 4 3 2 1
Printed in Canada

Text design by Acme Art, Inc.

Although Edward D. Wood, Jr. was his legal and preferred name,
the author was also known as Ed Wood, Jr. or Edw. D. Wood, Jr.

Killer in Drag

CHAPTER ONE

A man, wearing a bowler hat and a velvet trimmed greatcoat, left the grayish light of late afternoon to enter a side street drug store. Inside the poorly lighted establishment he paused to look around. The beady eyes in his pudgy, pink face searched for a telephone booth and when he located the object he moved immediately to it, pulled the glass door shut behind him then after depositing a coin in the proper slot, dialed a number. He waited impatiently, listening to spaced ringing at the other end. During its fourth ring the other end receiver was lifted.

"Yes?" The voice was almost too musical to be that of a man.

"Glen?" The man in the telephone booth talked near a whisper, almost as if he was afraid of being overheard. His eyes searched the store through a glass telephone booth window as he talked.

"Yes—This is Glen."

"Glenda is needed tonight."

"Where does she pick up her instructions?"

"Spot Seventeen—Ten o'clock."

"Got it."

After hearing the receiver on the other end click into silence, Pudgyface replaced his own receiver then walked quickly from the telephone booth, across the store and back out into the late afternoon pedestrian traffic.

CHAPTER TWO

Glen, a delicately formed youth, looked for several minutes at the telephone receiver, cussed himself silently for having accepted such a job on a cold night like this, then walked to his luxurious wall bar where he poured a stiff double shot of whiskey and downed it. The liquor sent much needed fire into his veins. He put the empty glass on the back-bar and crossed the expensive, effeminately decorated apartment. At the end table he pulled open the drawer revealing a dainty pearl handled automatic. He picked up the gun affectionately and slipped it smoothly into a pocket of the garment he was wearing. That garment was a fluffy, floor length, pink marabou negligee. Calmly, then, he made his way to the bedroom.

Mona, beautiful blonde Mona, sat on the edge of a rumpled king-sized bed waiting for him. She wore only a filmy nylon bed jacket which left nothing underneath to the imagination. Her eyes watched every move Glen made as he walked to a vanity table and removed his marabou negligee revealing beneath a pink satin, black lace trimmed nightgown. This he also took off, slipping it up over his head, and laying it across the vanity seat on top of the negligee.

"Going out?" Mona had begun to pout.

"Glenda has a job."

"Will you be gone long?"

"It's possible."

"Want me to leave?"

"You might get bored here alone."

"I don't think so."

"Can you get another date tonight?"

"I guess so. But I'd rather be with you."

"You'd better take the date. Be more interesting for you than sitting around here alone—with television."

The girl removed her bed jacket and tossed it to the bed then stepped into her panties as Glen left the room to enter the bathroom. Mona silently adjusted her brassiere then pulled a nylon slip down over her head. The sexy satin cocktail dress came next.

"Glen," she called lightly.

Glen did not answer because just at that moment he had flushed the toilet, drowning out her words. Mona waited for the sound to subside before she tried again.

"Glen!"

"Yes," he called from the other room.

"Can I borrow one of your coats—I'll get it back to you tomorrow?"

Glen appeared in the doorway, a terry towel wrapped around his middle. "Be sure to get it back by tomorrow."

"I always return anything I borrow when I say I will," she said, a bit injured.

"Sure—I know," he said, covering his words. "I'm sorry honey. Sure—take it. Not the silver blue mink though. I may need it."

Glen turned and was gone again into the bathroom. A moment later the sound of his

9

shower could be heard.

Mona fastened her pumps and walked to a closet which she opened. Inside were furs of every description. She selected a dark mink, slipped into it, closed the door and crossed the room.

"See you tomorrow Glen, honey," she called as she left the bedroom. But it was the noise of Glen's shower, this time, that closed her words from his ears.

CHAPTER THREE

It was cold. Dark clouds opened up permitting snowflakes to fall heavily through a bitter wind with dry streets quickly accepting the snow. By the time Glenda exited her apartment house a thick blanket of white had covered the ground. She stopped momentarily to pull the green satin hood of her fur-lined storm coat up over her head and the green angora beret perched there. The cop on the beat passed her silently, his eyes watching the sidewalk in front of him. Usually, when passing, the cop would send Glenda a sly wink and Glenda would reply with a flashing smile. This night the cop's mind must have been on other, more urgent, matters, not to have noticed her—as beautiful a picture as she presented.

Glenda gave the policeman only a brief second of consideration then walked off in an opposite direction. During the moment of time it had taken to adjust her coat hood she had thought of going to the parking lot for Glen's Cadillac convertible, but in the end decided against it. The "Spot-Seventeen" was such a short distance. She dug green angora glove covered hands deep into the coat pocket where her right hand fit snugly around the dainty pearl-handled .32.

Six blocks further on, the district changed to one of much less respectability than that where Glen lived. Glenda stopped in front of a dive called "Spot-Seventeen." She looked through the greasy window to see how many people were inside. Except for Jake the barkeep-owner, there were only four other persons in the room; two men at the bar and a frowzy big-titted blonde, snuggled around a wino in a front booth. Glenda pushed open the door and entered. She walked immediately to a rear booth where she took off her coat revealing a green angora sweater that matched the beret and green gabardine skirt. Glenda could really wear a sweater—and she usually did. Especially on jobs like this.

Jake made his way to the booth as she was hanging up her coat on a hook. "Evening, Miss— Ain't see'd you in a coupla weeks now."

Glenda only smiled as she seated herself.

"The usual?" he asked lightly.

Glenda nodded.

Jake moved away to return a moment later with a double martini which he put down in front of the green clad girl—green that seemed to match the color of her eyes.

"Got a mess out there tonight, ain't we?"

Glenda nodded as she automatically brushed back a lock of hair which had fallen from beneath her beret.

With a jerk of his thumb, Jack indicated the outside as he spoke again. "If rain hits that stuff's gonna slush up, then you can bet it'll be really lousy out there."

Glenda looked up at the lean, bony-faced man. Her eyes began to show annoyance at his persistence in trying to get her talking. Jake finally caught Glenda's look and realized its full meaning. He shrugged his shoulders and turned away. Glenda had been in "Spot-Seventeen" ten or twelve times and each time Jake had tried to strike up a conversation, but only once had she ever spoken to him. That was the first time she had come in. She had simply said, "A double martini, please." Then Glenda had smiled as if pleased with something she had said. Her voice was so sexily musical it had caused Jake to go home that night, to his wife, with extremely hot pants, and ever since that time he had tried in every way he knew to get this beautiful girl to speak again. But to this very moment she had not uttered another sound. However, he wasn't a man to give up hope. Here was a dream—a real dream—and those fuzzy angora sweaters she continually wore, gave her that mist-like quality of a real dream.

Jake was thus occupied in his thoughts when a little mouse-like character entered, looked around, then moved directly to Glenda's booth and sat down across the table from her. Jake made his way to them as Mouse was seating himself.

"What'll it be?"

"Scotch—on the rocks," ordered the Mouse.

Jake eyed Glenda as he spoke. "How about another for the lady?"

Mouse looked toward Glenda, his gaze a question. Glenda's eyes remained on her martini as she waved the bar-keep away with a movement of her hand.

Jake glanced at Mouse, then moved back

toward the bar.

"What's the job?" It was Glen's deep voice that came from between Glenda's lovely reddened lips.

"Wait'll he leaves again." The little man flicked his thumb toward Jake who was already on his way back to the table with a glass of scotch over ice.

"A dollar thirty," Jake said as he put the glass down in front of Mouse.

"Dollar thirty? What's in this scotch—platinum?" Mouse's eyes were hard as they met those of Jake.

"Dollar thirty fer both drinks. Yer's and the lady's."

"Wat' lady?—Ah—This broad makes more in one hour than I do in six months. Let 'er pay 'er own."

Glenda reached to her coat and pulled a billfold from the pocket. She removed two ones and put them into Jake's hand. The beautiful, long scarlet painted nails thrilled Jake's eyes. But Jake was in for a bigger thrill. "Keep it—both drinks." It was Glenda's voice again.

Four more words. Jake had heard four more words from those beautiful lips, from that lovely face, from that exotic creature. Jake's wife would sure catch hell that night. Jake even considered buying one of those fuzzy sweaters like Glenda was wearing, for his wife. Just considered it however, because almost immediately he had a mental picture of his wife wearing such a sweater—all two hundred pounds of her. Jake was shaking the horrible thought from his mind as Mouse spoke to him.

"Ya got yer tip—Whaddya' want—More?"

Jake scowled at Mouse then walked away, but as soon as he was behind the bar again his eyes became fastened across the room on Glenda's angora covered breasts and began to visualize her without anything on to distract his view. "Bet she's really got a pair of them stacked up there," he dreamed silently.

Glenda bit a tiny speck of olive from her tooth pick, then let the remainder fall back into the gin and vermouth filled glass. "Sometimes you talk too much, Mouse."

"Ahh. I ain't payin' fer no drinks fer no make believe dame. When I spring dough fer a dame's drink she can pay me back in bed doin' somethin' what only a real dame can shell out with."

"Mouse. It would be just as easy for the morgue boys to lay you out on a slab as any of my other clients."

"Only you wouldn't do nothin' like that, cause there ain't no money in it if you do me in. You ain't skeerin' me none . . . Ain't no fairy bastard like you ever skeered me . . ."

Glen clenched her fist, then reconsidered. "I can't have trouble with you—in here, Mouse, but the time will come. Mark my word. The time will come." Glenda's voice was low, but hard. A mixture of both hers and Glen's. But there was no mistaking the expression on her face. Glenda

15

was mad and could kill this Mousy creep with no more compunction than she would have stepping on a spider—perhaps less.

Mouse babbled on drunkenly as if not having heard. "All I know about you is what I can see—her." However he spoke softly so as not to be readily heard. "I know yer a man what makes up in girl's dresses and things. I ken' find fairies like you anyplace. Wanna know ten dives in this town, right now, where yer painted up friends—queer friends, hang out? Naw ya don't—cause ya already know them places . . ."

"All I want from you are the instructions you were to pass on to me."

Mouse dug a dirty envelope from his pocket. "Like always I'm to give ya this envelope, then ya puts twenty bucks in my palms. See—It's sealed!"

Glenda snatched the envelope from his grimy mitt, made sure the seal was unbroken, then took a twenty dollar bill from her wallet, tossed it to Mouse, then stood up and put on her coat.

The Mouse squeaked again. "Ain't ya gonna finish yer drink, Priddy girl?"

"You finish it!" As she spoke, Glenda picked up the martini and dashed the liquor into Mouse's startled face. Glenda adjusted the hood of her coat and walked swiftly from the bar.

Jake's eyes lingered for some time on the spot where he had last seen Glenda then realized Mouse again. Mouse's face still dripped from martini juice. Jake decided suddenly to throw the little worm out—he couldn't stand the sight of

16

him any longer. "After all," he thought. "That worm musta made some slimy remarks to have such a beautiful thing like that toss a martini in his face then stormin' outta my joint like that."

With blood in his eyes, Jake moved toward the Mouse.

CHAPTER FOUR

The rain had turned snow to slush as Glenda's cab pulled to a stop in front of a bleak Eastside tenement house with step down delicatessen in its basement. Glenda stepped, almost gingerly, through the slush to the sidewalk. The driver got out from his side and moved to Glenda. Both looked into the poorly lighted, product jammed, delicatessen window. Glenda was smiling, a weird smile, almost wicked.

"You sure look like you enjoy your work," said the cabbie.

"Sometimes I do." Glenda spoke softly, then added more pointedly, "I have a feeling there is a definite possibility I'll enjoy this one."

"You got something against this guy?"

"I've never even met him—I don't know him at all. But I will."

"Don't look like he's got no dough—anyway not enough for the syndicate gettin' hot over," reasoned the cabbie; a cabbie who had been designated where and when to meet in the sealed instructions Glenda had been given by the Mouse.

"You should spot his room during rush hours," Glenda had sneered her remarks. "Greenbaum, down there, is a real dyed in the wool welcher."

"Watch yourself—Maybe he ain't alone."

"My instructions said he'd be alone. I've yet to find my orders to be wrong."

"Just in case ya need outta here fast, I'll keep

the motor runnin'—huh?"

Glenda waited patiently while the Cabbie got behind the steering wheel of his cab, then she descended the stairs to the delicatessen.

A small overhead bell gave an off tune ring as she opened the door to enter. Greenbaum, a fat little man, came through a heavily curtained doorway at the rear of his establishment as Glenda walked to the counter near a large cash register. The little man moved to a position facing Glenda across the counter.

"Yes? "

"Greenbaum?"

"That is me—I can help you?" he asked.

"So my instructions tell me." It was Glen's voice—Hard.

The little Jewish proprietor looked dubiously at the pretty girl with the man's voice.

"Well—What is it?" He had to be sure. After all a sale was a sale.

"Maybe you'd like to suggest something?" It was Glen's voice again.

Now the little guy was sure of his thoughts. In his time he'd seen many of these queers running around in girl's clothes. Lots of them right there in his own neighborhood. They were bad medicine to have around and he wasn't having any. Maybe not many looked so pretty as this one in the fuzzy green hat and the green satin storm coat, but he had seen all of their kind he ever wanted to. Greenbaum didn't like their kind one damned bit.

"I ain't havin' none of you queers dressed up in girl's clothes in my store. So you should someplace go else before I call the coppers here yet."

Glenda's sweet, girlish voice answered. That radiantly, beautiful smile accompanied her words. There wasn't the slightest trace of Glen's voice in her tone. It was Glenda to the fullest extent of her being. So much so that the little bald headed, wrinkled man stepped back in astonishment, even before Glenda had pulled the dainty .32 from her coat pocket.

"I was hoping you'd say something like that. I hate to kill anyone I don't even know—especially if I don't know whether or not I like them. I'd rather have someone throw a dirty remark at me—then I hate and when I hate—It makes my position so much easier." She paused, then, "I'm a good shot."

The little man batted his eyes a couple of times. "Shoot—Shoot? What is this shoot business?"

Glenda moved the .32 a bit closer to the man. He took another step backward. "This is the kind of shoot to which I refer," replied Glenda pointedly, still with that beautiful smile.

"Eight dollars only I got in the till. Take it. But you should put that gun in the pocket back." He was shaking badly. "It might go off."

"I'm not interested in your eight dollars." Glen's voice again. Hard! Menacing! The beautifully painted face expressed no mercy. The green eyes bore holes in the frightened little man.

"What you want it is, then?"

"You!"

"Me?" The little eyes, becoming bloodshot now, batted again. "But, mine Got, I don't even know you. I don't ever have lay eyes on you."

"And you never will again. The big man stirred the capsules in a fish bowl and your number came up." Glenda's eyes narrowed. "When you arrive at the place you're going—if they have a syndicate—don't ever try to hold out on them. It'll only end up this same way."

"The?—The?—The syndicate? Why before you don't say you're from the syndicate. I'm sorry I make such bad things at you. Such bad jokes. What ever the syndicate does is right. Is fine by me. Sure—Sure—Look! You don't gotta shoot. I got the money. Right here . . . ?" He pointed to a drawer beside the cash register. "And—and— The joke—I didn't know. You must forget what I said, huh?—Sure—The money I got right here in—" He once more pointed to the drawer beside his cash register.

"Open it—If you try for a gun I'll see you go out the hard way. Right in the belly where it'll hurt—where it'll take you a long time to die."

"No gun! I don't got a gun in there—Not even in the store I ain't got no gun. Only money there is in." His hand pulled open the drawer and drew out a bank money sack. Glenda's beautiful eyes watched him carefully as he tossed the bag quickly onto the counter. "Two thousand dollars is there." He wet his very dry lips. "My wife. She needed an operation. I have to keep money a while. I mean to pay up to the syndicate." Greenbaum pointed to the money sack again. "This proves it. Don't it? The operation she needed bad. But my life, I need too. There is money. Take it! Madam—Mister—Miss—You go—You will go and not shoot me—huh?" He was pleading violently, tears in his eyes.

Glenda picked up the money bag with her free hand. "Operations I don't know about, and I care less." She slipped the money bag into her purse. "I only know you still owe the syndicate two grand which you haven't paid."

"Paid?—I just paid—I paid the two grands."

"So you say—But who can prove it?"

"But—but—but—I just paid." Greenbaum got it. His face went into shock. "Ah—Mine Got—You sneak—You fairy bastard—I know what you try to pull—You pulled a cross double. I tell the syndicate—You lie—I pay and you take it—I prove it to them. . . ."

Glenda cut in swiftly. "Dead men don't tell anything, nor do they prove much except that maybe they're dead."

It was Glenda's sweet musical voice that spoke the last words the little man was to ever hear on this earth. The dainty .32 blasted twice. The first two bullets hit the man squarely in the neck. The shock caused his eyes to snap cross-eyed, then the lids closed out his fearful look.

Glenda fired the third shot into the little man's

lower jaw as the man was failing to the floor
behind his counter.

CHAPTER FIVE

Glenda decided to wear a new, long sleeved, white turtle neck angora sweater for the occasion. It wasn't every day one in her station of life could be invited to the swank Dalten Van Carter's apartment. Dalten Van Carter could be instrumental in causing Glenda's greatest desire to be fulfilled. He knew all the important people in the city; the world, for that matter. And it had been Dalten Van Carter who had actually extended her a dinner invitation.

For some time Glen had been investigating the possibilities of quitting his professional assassin affairs. With each new assignment the wear on his nerves became more prominent. He was getting weary of killing. At first it had been a thrill, a great challenge, but lately it had begun to bore him. All along it had been a means of getting the great amounts of ready cash he needed for his future plan. A plan which must be carried out soon, while he was still young enough to enjoy it to the fullest extent. He would soon have enough to carry him over for a long time.

He felt continually, more and more strongly, that his counterpart, Glenda was much more suited to better things in life than just that of a hired killer.

Sometimes at night he would awaken in a cold sweat; a sweat which drenched Glenda's expensive nightgowns. The faces of his victims were visiting him more and more frequently. Dalten

Van Carter could direct Glen to the better, less trying way of life.

True, Dalten Van Carter was a real Grandma type homosexual, but after all, the man did have money and connections. Connections, Glen had learned early in life, were the most important thing in life other than money itself. Without connections there never could be money— enough money.

Glen realized he had a good cash stake right there in his apartment. Eleven thousand dollars which included the two grand picked up a few days before when Glenda knocked off the old man. That kind of money could take him from the syndicate if Dalten Van Carter would fix him the spot. But it must be done in just the right way—after all—the syndicate didn't approve of anyone quitting on them—especially ones who knew as much as he and Glenda knew. Both Glen and Glenda could well vouch for what happens to quitters. Perhaps after a few nights with Dalten Van Carter the entire plan would present itself. When it did, Glen knew he would be ready. At least it was worth a try, even if Glenda did have to shack up with the wrinkled old millionaire a few weeks. The syndicate had a long arm, but after the operation which would make Glenda a real girl, she could well disappear forever from their grasp. Oh the ecstasy of it. The love of life Glen felt when he realized, soon it would be possible to be the girl he had always dreamed of himself being. Never again would he have to attire himself in the horror of men's attire. Dalten Van Carter would know of a place he could go; of a doctor who would be willing to perform the change surgery. All Glen had to do was be Glenda and Glenda be nice to Dalten Van Carter.

The beautiful angora sweater fitted snugly over a black velvet skirt at her hips. A matching black velvet belt with a rhinestone buckle embraced tightly to her twenty-two inch waist line and the angora sweater was pulled tightly through the belt, giving her a long but properly curved line effect. Glenda's specially made breast pads stood out as beautifully as any sweater model's breasts. Her glamorous blonde wig was topped with a snowy white angora beret.

Glenda looked for a long time in the mirror of her vanity table before she got up and walked across a soft white fur rug to the bedroom closet where she selected a three quarter length white fox coat and slipped into it. Then she went back to the vanity table and stuffed her black velvet shoulder strap bag full of the little feminine necessities and including her wallet which also held money and Glen's identification. At all times she carried at least a couple of hundred dollars in a hidden recess of the purse and Glen's identification always went with her. If she were caught in "drag" like this, the authorities could be very strict about such things as proper identification. The judge would go easier on anyone with the right sex on their papers.

Looking into the vanity table mirror again,

Glenda dabbed a dry cotton pad to the corner of her beautifully made up eyes, then fished into her purse for a lipstick brush. Holding the brush expertly in her hand she touched the corners of her lips then smiled at the lovely reflection who smiled back at her.

She was ready. She hooked her fur coat, adjusted the long purse strap over her shoulder and walked out of the bedroom. As her black velvet pumps carried her through the doorway, she paused only long enough to turn off the lights via a wall switch.

Several persons smiled warmly at this tall, lovely girl, as she walked through the apartment lobby. All of them had seen her before, but always she had disappeared before they could strike up even the slightest acquaintanceship or conversation. Once a bellboy had actually followed her successfully to the eighth floor, the floor Glen lived on, but then she had disappeared like a vapor of smoke. One thing was sure. This lovely creature wasn't registered at this Apartment-Hotel.

The same bellboy now leaned across the shiny marble top to a desk clerk, but did not take his eyes from those sensational rolling hips as they crossed the polished tile lobby.

"Who's she shackin' with Herb?" the bellboy asked.

"How should I know? I don't butt into what ain't none of my business," replied the desk clerk. However, even he couldn't take his eyes from the rear of the white fur covered girl, nor could he stop his mind from visualizing texture and movement of that soft flesh under the fur coat.

"Yeah—Guess you're right. Keep your nose out of other people's business and it keeps its shape longer—The nose I mean."

"Anyway," mentioned the desk clerk further, "Why ask me. You got to the eighth floor with her once, didn't you?"

The bellboys eyes lighted up suddenly. "Yeah," he replied dreamily. "It was summer—She was wearing pink slacks and a pink sweater. Not one of them fuzzy kind like she's got on now—but a tight one; showed just about everything she had. I'll never forget that sight if I live to be a thousand. Let me tell you. That set of titties she's got sure does stretch the wool—and the imagination— WHOW."

Glenda left the apartment house and entered the streets. A night beat cop saluted her with his billy club and Glenda winked slyly over her winning smile. This time she was sure the cop was feeling sensations to his very core; sensations that he would never admit to another human being, especially to his devoted wife waiting for him at home with dinner.

Glenda turned left at the corner then half way along the street she jay walked across to a parking lot where Glen kept his light blue Cadillac convertible which was stalled at the far end of the lot. Glenda liked that. Glen never did. But Glenda appreciated the longer walk; she enjoyed hearing those high heels click on hard cement. She could, and many times did, walk for miles just listening to her spike heels as they clicked along rhythmically.

She slid behind the steering wheel. For a long moment her hand rested on the convertible top release as she tried to decide whether to leave the top up or electrically put it down. A sudden chill shook her frame and the hand came swiftly away from the top release. She pulled the collar of her fur coat tighter around her neck. The convertible top was up to stay.

She put her car into motion. If she hadn't had excellent brakes, she would have run down a young parking lot attendant, who charged out in front of the car. The attendant came swiftly around to her window and stuck his pock-marked, ugly head into the window.

"What's with you, broad? Maybe you ain't got the right car?" he sneered.

An older attendant moved up and tapped his youthful parker on the back. The young man withdrew his head; looked quizzically up at the man. The old timer smiled broadly and motioned Glenda to move on. "Sorry to have delayed you, Miss Satin."

Glenda flashed him that warm smile and drove the Cadillac out into traffic. When she had gone the older man faced his pock-marked assistant angrily. "You tryin' to lose one of my best customers?—A monthly yet?"

"That car don't belong to that broad." He spoke hard, pointedly.

"Sure it don't, Ace, but that car does belong to Glen Marker an' he says she's to get it anytime she's got the keys to start it with."

Glenda obeyed all the traffic signals. This was the only place she could ever fail in her impersonation. Glen had never gotten a driver's license in Glenda's name. Of course she always carried Glen's license, but she would undoubtedly be in a difficult situation should she ever have to present it.

In all other things Glenda was pleased with herself and all the things Glen could do for her. Even deciding to buy the angora sweater she now wore had been the right decision. It had been very expensive, but so had the green satin cocktail dress which she had worn to a party for a supposedly influential man who turned out to be a society bum. Those things were all fortunes of war—expensive clothes—uniforms of her trade.

The evening held a true chill and a definite promise of a cold fog and probably more snow. The angora sweater had by far been the best choice for warmth and looks. "Angora," she said aloud. "What a delightful sound. What a magnificent feeling." She opened one hook on her fur coat and let her right hand entered the opening. A pleasant sensation surged through her body as the hand felt the soft angora fur which surrounded her left breast. She squeezed harder—then harder—she rubbed it—the sensation overwhelmed her—She sighed aloud—"Oh what matter—there are more panties in the glove

30

compartment."

Half an hour later Glenda parked her Cadillac across from the Crenshaw Arms apartments, locked it almost gaily, crossed the street toward the building. She flashed a beautiful smile at the red and gold coated doorman who saluted her in return, then she entered the building.

To say that Glenda walked across the spacious lobby to an elevator is not enough. Glenda didn't just walk. Watching her was to feel the pleasant roll of a luxury liner; the smooth flow of an airplane high in the altitudes, entering silent drifts of white cloud puffs over a clear day. She moved as though she were an angel or a specter in a wonderful dream.

Glenda removed her fur coat even before the elevator doors opened and placed it over her arms. She fluffed up the fur of her sweater then pulled it tighter across her, not too big, not too small, but definitely pointed breasts. She stepped lightly into the elevator as the door opened. The elevator boy, a man of at least Sixty-five, couldn't seem to close his eyes or take them away from this exquisite, tall, sweater-clad girl. He watched her enter. He watched her every swaying movement. He was entranced with her. He kept his eyes glued where most men, even at his advanced age, would generally look.

"What floor, Miss?" he finally stammered. She told him but he made no move toward the controls.

Finally, Glenda, with a flash of her lovely smile,

reached behind the old man and pushed the penthouse button. The old man's eyes remained glued on the angora clad girl, the like of which he didn't often see anymore even with his job of transporting people all day and many nights. He didn't even realize the doors had closed behind them and the carriage was swiftly rising.

The doors opened again at the penthouse hallway. The little man appeared to be gasping for air. Glenda felt sure this little man would retire to the men's room in the basement for several moments as soon as he could get clear of his elevator; so she kissed him quickly on his high forehead, leaving a big red smear of lipstick. She felt sure her kiss, and its remaining imprint, would help him later in what he would have to do.

CHAPTER SIX

Dalten Van Carter was an old man, a very old man, who drank too much and he thought too much of feverish, perverted sex. He flounced around his apartment like a fluttering old auntie, like a nymph in a flower bed; a fairy in the scented woodlands. He wore a faded pink satin wrapper which was trimmed in ancient, almost decaying, white fox—reminiscent of his much younger days. He didn't try to cover up the fact that at one time he had been as beautiful a "drag" as Glenda was now. Pictures on the walls proved that point very well. But strain of all the fuss and bother of using make-up and the placement of wigs and girdles and other specialized devices to hide unwanted pieces of male anatomy were too much to bother with these past few years. In most cases, around the apartment now, he simply wore one of his satin briefs with an extra large bulky type brassiere, and a selection from his faded wrappers. One thing Dalten Van Carter kept beautiful at all times were his fingernails. Long, well-tended nails. Smooth as any woman's nails; painted a bright scarlet.

The aged "drag's" eyes all but popped their sockets when they lighted on Glenda as she glided into the room. He stepped back in amazement—awed at the beauty of the "girl" he beheld. He had seen a lot of them in his day but this was by far the loveliest thing he had ever laid eyes on. He shut the door without removing his eyes from her and when the door was closed he took three studied tours around her, looking her up and down and muttering. "Exquisite. Beautiful. Sensational. Ohhh—This will be grand." He was thinking of later . . .

Then he stopped his gleeful study to face her. "You are all I've heard you to be, Glenda."

"Thank you." It didn't sound good. Too much of Glen's deep tones. Glenda must start working on her voice again.

"But here I am forgetting my manners already. Come in. Come in. Put your coat on the chair— Wilma, my maid, will take care of it. What do you drink, my dear?" All the time Van Carter talked he walked and the fur at his wrapper hem line trailed out behind him. "Dear me, girl, had I really fully realized how beautiful you'd be, I'd have taken more pains in my attire."

"Are you comfortable?" Glenda asked diplomatically with a raised eyebrow.

"Well—I should think so."

"Good. So am I. We are dressed as we feel best for our own comfort."

"You dear thing."

The evening wore on quickly. Dinner was served by Wilma, a Negro boy flawlessly dressed in a short skirted maid's outfit of black satin, then Dalten prepared several more drinks which Glenda and he consumed slowly. Dalten had to show the costumes he had in his wardrobe— "From my better years," he had explained. He opened his pink wrapper to show black lace

34

panties with pink bows.

Then suddenly, it was one thirty in the morning.

"You of course will stay the night dear Glenda?"

"If you'd like."

"If I like—I insist darling thing. I'm dying for you to stay."

"Maybe I should have brought an overnight bag."

"Nonsense. I have everything you'll need."

"You are prepared for guests?"

"I've been at this for some seventy *odd* years. What is your favorite color, darling?"

"Pink," answered Glenda softly.

Dalten was out of his chair like a shot. He disappeared into a bedroom for a moment then he was back carrying a pink satin nightgown with a matching negligee and pink fur mules. He handed them to Glenda.

"You'll find a dressing area adjoining my bedroom. Oh never fear—The nightie and all those things are brand new. None of my guests go away without a little gift which might delight them. And you were very special even before I laid eyes on you. Our mutual friend Paul knew your size and thought you might prefer pink. I bought several other colors however, just in case. Besides—I hope this is only the first of many visits, my darling."

Glenda squeezed the old man's hand affectionately. She liked him already; genuinely liked him.

She didn't, however, relish the idea of sharing the bed with him; his aged wrinkled body, but one word from Dalten Van Carter and there were no heights in the world too difficult to attain. Glen's possibility of escaping the syndicate forever became more evident—more important and attainable.

"Hurry now—Go dress." Dalten Van Carter giggled almost childishly. "Or should I say un-dress."

Glenda got up slowly to enter a prearranged bedroom, then continued on into the perfumed dressing room which occupied that space between bedroom and bathroom. When she had slipped out of her warm clothing and into the sheer pink nightgown, she felt a quick chill. She hugged her arms closely about her for several moments until the chill was gone and warm blood returned to her veins. After that she selected one of the many bottles of perfume from the vanity and dipped the stopper deep into the bottle then applied the sweetened mixture behind each ear, also not forgetting the place above each of her foam rubber breasts. She lifted the negligee from the back of the vanity stool and slipped into it. She tied a large bow at the top surveyed herself in a full length mirror on the bathroom door. She smiled, pleased. A soft, luscious body greeted her eyes through the thin pink material as the negligee opened slightly. She pushed the left side far back and put her hand on her hip. The negligee, partly open, revealed so much more of her tempting body. She slipped her feet into the pink fur mules and pushed open the bedroom door with her free right hand.

Dalten Van Carter, nude, in bed, the blankets pulled up tightly under his chin squealed with delight as he watched her glide into the room. His gleeful squeal became almost uncontrollable as he watched her slip so elegantly, so sexily, every movement with meaning, out of the negligee. She tossed the sheer garment across the foot of the bed and for a long moment the light behind her came through the material of her matching nightgown. Every curve of her luscious body was naked to the eye beneath the filmy nightgown; almost as if she were clothed in a faint pink mist. Dalten Van Carter saw in a flash that she wore no panties beneath that pink mist. His hand shot to the light switch at his bedside. The room fell captive to the darkness.

"Please come to me." Dalten Vin Carter's voice was painful, strained. Passionate. Tormented.

Glenda slid softly into the bed beside the old man. Immediately he was at Glenda. She felt his hot breath on her neck; her ears; her throat; her hair. He wiggled. He squirmed. Sweat poured from his sex hungry body. He moaned words of endearment. Words of love; of forever worship. His hand suddenly lashed out and tore the right shoulder strap from Glenda's nightie. Then the left hand tore the other strap. The foam rubber breasts that made many women green with jealousy, rolled from her flat chest to lose themselves

37

in the fast becoming wrinkled sheets and blankets. Dalten Van Carter's tongue searched the small boyish nipples of her breasts as his feverish hands pushed away the pink mist.

Lights suddenly flooded the room. Glenda's hands automatically pulled the blanket up over Dalten and herself. Dalten moved sheepishly up from under the blankets. He was shaking. His passion gone. Both stared at the thin man in the doorway across the room.

"Karl!" exclaimed the old man. Terror in his voice. It was more of a hiss than a word. It was all he could say at the moment and he had no more time to think of anything.

The man in the doorway took a snub nosed revolver from his pocket. He fired six times into Dalten Van Carter's body from the doorway where he stood. The first bullet had been enough. It caught Dalten Van Carter in the center of his wrinkled forehead. The others simply pressured themselves into the lifeless flesh. The blood from each impact splattered over Glenda. She screamed loud, high pitched, as a girl in fright, in startled terror.

The little man turned his gun on Glenda as if fully realizing her presence for the first time. His finger pressed repeatedly on the trigger but each time the hammer fell on an empty chamber with little, but frightening, metallic clicks. The man suddenly turned and ran into the Negro who had come running. Both went to the floor. The man pushed the Negro out of the way as he got to his feet and was gone as quickly as he had appeared.

The Negro, wearing a tong flannel nightgown and robe, got to his feet and raced into the room. He paused momentarily, taking in the situation at a glance.

Glenda lay as before, staring at the spot where the man had been. The Negro rushed to her and pulled the bed clothes out of her hands. He had to force her hands loose.

"You'd better get outta here fast Miss Glenda. Them shots is gonna bring all the cops in town up here quick like a bunny."

Glenda couldn't bring herself to move or speak. The material of her nightgown fell into a circle around her feet as the Negro frantically pulled her out of bed. The pink material fell as she stood up.

"Hurry—Hurry, Missy Glenda, the cops." But he saw the girl's apparent state of deep shock. He lashed out with the flat of his hand to strike her across the face several times. The slaps resounded throughout the room.

Glenda had been a dealer in death a long time. But never before had she been so close to it herself. The gun had been pointed at her. Only an empty chamber had saved her life. Her life and Glen's.

Glenda came to her senses. She raced into the dressing room and frantically pulled on her undies then her skirt. The Negro came into the room on the run. He held out the bust pads which Glenda quickly stuffed into the vacant cups of her brassiere.

"Mistah Karl done it this time. Mistah Karl done killed Mistah Dalten. Mistah Dalten chucked him outta here ta other day. Done with him he said . . . Didn't take the key away from him. You gotta get goin' Miss Glenda—Quick outta heah . . ."

Glenda slipped into her angora sweater as the Negro raced out of the room again. She adjusted the velvet belt then sat down to slip into and fasten her pump straps securely around her ankle. She quickly took up her beret then ran through the bedroom to the living room. The Negro held her coat. She grabbed it and raced toward the front door.

"Not that way. They's already been poundin' on that door. Get out the back way."

He ushered her quickly through the kitchen and out the rear exit. The door led to the roof and a fire ladder down to the next floor. A fire ladder is a dangerous thing at times, but in high heels, even more so, but Glenda tackled and conquered it immediately, without even a thought as to any other danger than that which was behind her in the satin covered canopy bed.

Once on the floor below, she found the service elevator and took it to the basement. No one greeted her as she stepped out into the damp basement. She looked around cautiously then made for the service entrance. For the moment a thought went through her mind as to where the elevator operator was—then it occurred that it was very late—he had probably gone off duty by this time.

As she opened the door, cool air from an alley greeted her, miraculously clearing her head. She heard a distant siren. Too distant to be a menace at the moment. Quickly she slid into her coat and pulled it tightly around her then raced to the alley entrance where she cautiously entered the street.

Glenda crossed the cement and unlocked Glen's Cadillac. She slid in behind the wheel. As the automobile moved into action the police car, siren screaming, raced past her, coming in from a direction toward her. It screeched to a stop in front of the Crenshaw Arms apartments. Before she had turned the corner she saw four uniformed policemen and a plainclothesman get out of the police car and move with determined steps into the building.

Glenda drove the Cadillac slowly for several blocks then gave it the gun.

CHAPTER SEVEN

It was a sigh of great relief Glenda expounded as she parked Glen's Cadillac in the parking lot. Exhausted from the terror she'd been through she leaned back against the soft cushion of the driver's seat. The release of tension encased her whole being. Little beads of sweat dotted her forehead. It glistened against her make-up.

She needed a cleansing tissue.

There were plenty of them in her purse on the seat beside her where she always kept it. Cleansing tissue was a necessary item when one depended upon as much make-up as she did. Glenda reached for the purse.

The purse wasn't there.

The tension returned rapidly; took hold of Glenda's whole body; it froze her into a rigid state of near shock. Her head became dizzy; she strained against sudden tightening muscles. Her movement was quick. She frantically searched the seat, the floor boards; between the seats. Then it hit her. Hit her as plainly as if the picture were being projected on the windshield in front of her; like on the screen at a drive–in movie theater.

"The scene: INTERIOR DRESSING ROOM— VAN CARTER APARTMENT. A black velvet purse on a neat vanity table. Reflected in the mirror, through the opened door can be seen policemen in the next room as they go about the usual business of a murder investigation."

Glenda jumped out of the car and slammed the

door. Her high heels made the fast click-click on the cement as she raced to Glen's apartment building. Breathlessly she entered the lobby and made it quickly to the elevator area.

There was no operator on duty, so she got in the elevator and pushed the eighth floor button. The door automatically closed behind her and the elevator shot upward.

At Glen's apartment door she hurriedly inserted a key and entered. Luckily she had put her ring of keys in her fur coat pocket before entering Dalten Van Carter's place. Glenda slammed the door and raced to her bedroom where she quickly took off the clothes she wore, all but her pink panties and brassiere which she left on for the moment. She sat down at a well lighted vanity and took out several bottles and cream jars.

Ten minutes later, Glen, using a heavy towel, wiped the last of the cold cream from his face and stood up. He took the wig and laid it on the bed then took Glenda's brassiere and falsies off. He let them fall to the bed. He moved to his closet and selected a brown suit and white shirt which he quickly put on. Then his shoes and socks were hastily slipped into and a brown tie knotted about his neck. When he was fully dressed he pulled a large suitcase down from a closet shelf. He stuffed it with a gray suit and a set of blue suede shoes and a shaving kit. He raced across the room to Glenda's wardrobe where he selected a fur jacket; a light blue and two pair of pumps, one set in black and the other a street suit; a beige jersey dress; a pair of beige slacks in gray; as well as a third set of beige low heel walking shoes. From the dresser drawer, he took two sweater sets, both in soft wool; one beige and the other pink. Then over these he packed his wig; several pair of panties and brassieres. He put the brassieres, falsies and the turtle neck angora sweater he had just taken off into the suitcase on top of the other things then closed the lid. On his way out of the room he took his spare wallet from the drawer; put it in his pocket, then from the same drawer, hidden beneath a secret drawer bottom, he took out several bundles of bills and stuffed them into the inside pocket of his jacket.

As Glen reached the darkness of his living room he was stopped by a pounding on the door, followed by an official voice muffled through the thick hardwood.

"Open up in there. This is the police."

Glen turned, slipped silently back into his bedroom, then on into the bathroom. He shoved up a window and climbed out onto a fire escape. He was like a mad man as he carelessly raced down the iron steps. When he reached the alley below, he heard the yells of the police far above him. But for the moment he felt out of danger. A moment later and he reached his Cadillac in the parking lot and another thirty seconds he had the Cadillac well on the road toward the state highway.

Glen's mind seemed to move as fast as the state highway beneath the Cadillac's rolling wheels. He wasn't quite sure this was really happening to him. It seemed more like one of those bad dreams. But it was happening. He had felt the warm blood of a murder victim as the blood splattered on his face. Even more. He was the one hunted. After all the crimes he had actually committed he was trapped by one that he had had no part in. His double identity was sure to be found. He *had* been in Dalten Van Carter's bedroom, in his very bed when it happened. He had been Glen in Glenda's clothing. The police would know. They would find him. Glen's identification was in that velvet purse. They would find the blood soaked circle of pink nightgown at the foot of the bed where he had let it lay when it fell around his feet. They would grill the colored boy until he told them everything he knew; everything that had gone on in that apartment prior to the murder. Maybe they couldn't touch him for the murder. But everything else would be lost. Glen and Glenda would be known. He would be of no further use to the syndicate. No one remained a part of the syndicate if they were of no use to them. All they received was a big, all expense paid, funeral.

The newspapers would have a field day with this one.

Glen thought of Glenda's beautiful, expensive wardrobe he had to leave behind in the apartment. The dresses; the sweater; the suits; blouses; nighties; negligees; robes; lingerie; shoes. All that he had worked so hard to acquire. Any policeman worth his salt would know the whole story one minute after he walked into that apartment. Almost before the lights had been put on they would know. Glenda had so loved the scent of perfume. The apartment was drenched in perfume. And the cops were there now.

Glen reached at his pocket to make sure he had secured his spare wallet and identification there. It was. And then he felt too the bulge under his right arm where the wad of money rested. He felt better. At least he wouldn't be stranded along the road someplace without cash.

Then it hit him. A realization he should have gotten before. If he was to keep his Cadillac it was only a matter of time until he was picked up. Surely they would send out a description of it. He had always kept a miniature license plate under the flap of his wallet near his driver's license. The police would have also found that by now.

Ten miles out of town Glen turned off the main highway and hit a lesser used back road. He stayed on this dark, almost country like road for an hour, then he made a sharp left turn, sending his car into some deep brush beside the road. The motor stalled before the Cadillac's long rear end was off the soft shoulder. Glen cursed aloud, and with some difficulty he restarted the motor then pushed the gear into low. The car shot forward into a thick tangle of weeds. The Cadillac smacked head on into a tree some twenty-five yards off the road. The jungle like brush entanglement seemed to spring into action to cover the car almost as soon as it had stopped. Glen reached to the rear seat and took up his heavy suitcase. He followed the path made by the Cadillac, to the road. He looked back once, toward where the Cadillac was hidden. He sighed, almost as Glenda would have done, then after shrugging his shoulders he started the long hike up the dark, very deep rutted country like road.

CHAPTER EIGHT

It was ten thirty in the morning as Glen emerged from the old road into a small country village which seemed to be an Eastern version of an early Western cow town. He had walked the miserable dusty road throughout the night. He had stumbled in the ruts often and a few times had fallen to his knees, tearing one of his trouser legs. His clothing was as soiled as if he had been on the road for days instead of only a few hours. The old road ended at a highway near the edge of the village.

Glen approached the sleepy little place cautiously. There were only a few farmerish looking men and women and a couple of old cars on the single main street. He walked up onto the board walk then set his suitcase down to give himself a moment's rest. His arms ached. His back ached. As his red rimmed eyes searched the wooden structures he flexed his aching muscles. The strained eyes came to rest on a beaten, tired looking cafe sign which caused him to realize it had been many hours since he had last eaten. He bent over and picked up his suitcase again; crossed the street and entered a copper bound swinging door.

The inside of the cafe looked just as tired as the outside. The seating arrangement held a set of twelve stools lined up, almost evenly, at a scarred counter. A waitress, all two hundred pounds of her, waddled from a greasy kitchen to face him as he seated himself on the stool nearest the door.

Her face screwed up distastefully as she watched him pick up a menu—a typed sheet of paper on a cardboard backing, and began to read the short list of possible wants.

She waited long enough. "So what'd ya want?" Her voice matched the ugliness of her body and pock marked face. She pushed her dirty gray hair back as it fell ungracefully into her eyes.

Glen didn't look to the woman as he ordered. He tossed the menu back to the counter. "Ham and eggs. Coffee and toast. Light."

"Light what?"

"Light toast."

"So what's that?"

"Don't make the toast too dark."

"Buster. We got only one way to make toast and that's the way the electric toaster pops it out." Her hands were held defiantly on her hips.

"Then would you mind putting the butter on as soon as it comes out of the toaster?" Glen's eyes had slowly turned up to look at her.

"You sure are a fussy one for a road tramp." She had sneered the remark.

"Road tramp?" Glen looked down at his clothing. He did look like a road tramp at that. "Yeah. Guess I am at that." He tried for a smile.

"You got a dollar twenty-five to pay with?"

She turned her back on Glen before he could answer. She took down a large mug from the shelf and filled it with the steaming coffee from an urn, then shoved the cup in front of Glen. "Cause if you ain't," she indicated the coffee, "that's all you

49

get in this place. I can't support no road tramps any more than that—A cup of java."

Glen reached to his back pocket and took out his wallet. Always he had kept a twenty dollar bill in the spare wallet, just in case. To drag out his big wad certainly wouldn't be the thing to do even though he'd like to do just that, just to see the face of this ugly broad.

The waitress made a face at the twenty as Glen pocketed the money again.

"Who'd you roll?" A last sneer.

She walked away to the kitchen. A moment later she opened the kitchen door again and stuck her head out. "Want the morning paper to look at while the stuff cooks up?"

"This morning's paper?"

"We ain't so far out in the sticks, buster."

"Big town or your town's paper?"

"Big town. Comes in on the five a.m. bus. Look buster. I'm only tryin' to be a right guy with you. If you don't want the paper you don't have to look at it."

"I'd like to see it."

She tossed a rolled and tied up paper to the counter in front of him. "Don't tear it up, I ain't had time to look at it yet." She let the door swing shut behind her and was gone again.

Glen took up the roll of paper, broke the string and spread the paper out in front of him. His fingers trembled in the movement. The thick black headlines hit him squarely in the face. "DALTEN VAN CARTER MURDERED." The story line read: "Wealthy Stock Broker, Dalten Van Carter was found shot to death in the bedroom of his luxurious penthouse apartment. Glen Marker, a man of dubious income is being sought for questioning in connection with the killing as his identification was discovered in a woman's black velvet purse, found in Van Carter's dressing room. Only one clue was a pink night gown found beside the bed. JoJo Burnside, youthful Negro valet to Van Carter was found some moments later in a hall closet. His throat had been slashed . . ." continued on page two.

Glen turned the page. He eyes opened wide. He slammed the page shut. A three column eight inch picture of himself had come to his eyes. Glen crumpled the paper, but keeping it in his hand, picked up his suitcase and raced from the food joint.

Glen ran through the little village and continued running up the state highway until his lungs seemed ready to burst from within his chest. Then he found himself standing, resting, on a small state constructed bridge. Over the side he could see a narrow brook. He looked both ways on the road; with no cars coming either way, he climbed down the embankment and hid himself beneath the bridge.

For a long moment he sat in the cool shade. His mind tried to pick up the loose ends. Surely he would be discovered before he got very far with his picture plastered all over the papers.

Suddenly he tore open the paper. He read

partly aloud, as if something he had read before suddenly had hit him. "JoJo Burnside, youthful Negro valet to Van Carter was found some moments later in a hall broom closet. His throat had been slashed."

Glen closed the paper slowly.

The little Negro boy who had helped him escape was also dead. Murdered! The only one, other than the murderer, who knew that Glenda had not killed Van Carter.

Glen stared into nothingness. His mind traveled back to the events of the previous night.

The little Negro boy had been alive when Glenda had left the apartment. But how could the murderer have returned when the police had already been knocking at the door. No that couldn't be possible either. Glenda had seen the police arrive. Arrive after she was out of the building and already in Glen's Cadillac. Somebody else had been banging on that door. The murderer had returned.

The poor little jerk. He'd thought it was the cops. He'd helped Glenda to get away, then returned to open the door to permit death its entrance.

Glen had run all night so as not to be caught as a "drag." Now he also had to run from a murderer's tag.

Glen sunk back among the bridge support. He let the newspaper fall into the brook and it floated out of sight down stream. Glen closed his eyes for just a moment. Just one small moment to help rid himself of the vision and dizziness he felt quickly overcoming him. Just for one small moment he would close his eyes. Four hours later, stiff from the damp earth he had been laying on, but much more rested, Glen opened his eyes. He bolted upright, standing, blinking his eyes. He looked at his watch. Ten thirty in the morning. But rested, Glen knew what he had to do. He took a crumpled pack of cigarettes from his pocket, lighted one and inhaled deeply. The smoke, strong in his lungs, felt good.

Glen seated himself again, pulled the suitcase to him and began to fumble with the straps.

They had Glen's picture—but they did not have that of Glenda. It was impossible. Glenda had never had a photograph taken of himself.

CHAPTER NINE

Some twenty minutes later Glenda emerged from underneath the bridge. She wore the beige slacks and yellow sweater set with the three quarter length fur jacket over all. The long auburn hair of her wig tumbled freely down into the fur of the jacket. Glenda had only a small purse mirror by which to make-up but the make-up felt good so she knew it was flawless.

She looked to the sun; almost at the same time she unhooked her fur jacket. It was getting very warm, nothing like one would expect on a winter day. It was more like a day in the middle of spring. She took off the fur, looped it over one arm and with the other picked up her suitcase.

It was still a long way to California.

CHAPTER TEN

The suitcase had become heavy in her hand. Her long, well painted fingernails, a deep scarlet that matched her lip rouge, dug into the palm of her hand as her fingers encircled the suitcase grip. She had walked a full three hours when she thought of setting the suit case down for a moment's rest. But at that point she heard the chug-chug of an old motor behind her. She put the suitcase down; turned to face the oncoming vehicle; if it could at all be called that. At least it did have four so called wheels and a battered square body. It was something which could be ridden in. Glenda's bright scarlet lips parted to show even teeth in a broad come on smile. A smile as warm as a lover's kiss. The smile that had wilted so many a man to her wishes. The smile that seemed to promise caresses that were never to be realized.

The old Ford chugged to a stop. The farmer behind the wheel wasn't much more than forty years old, but because of an unshaven face and the dirty weather beaten clothes he wore; as dirty as the interior of the car; he gave the impression of being much older. The man leaned his great hulk across the empty seat to his right and snapped open the door.

"Jump in girlie," the farmer called, showing yellow tobacco stained teeth in a grizzly grin.

"Thanks mister." Glenda's voice was musical. She'd like to say more. She'd like to hear her voice again. Maybe she didn't have to consult a voice coach after all.

The farmer had difficulty jamming the gear into place. "God danged old heap has gotta go one of these days comin' along soon." Then the car jumped forward.

"At least it's transportation," Glenda said and with a quick gesture, brushed the left side of her yellow cardigan back from her breast. This movement caused the yellow wool of the slip-over sweater to be pushed out in a neat little ball with a sharp pointed tip.

The farmer watched her every movement from the corner of his eyes. Sweat began to show on his grimy brow. He wet his suddenly dry lips with the end of his tongue. Watching her move that yellow sweater around gave him an even greater thrill than he had first witnessed when he saw her standing on the road hitching a ride. His jaws moved faster as he chewed the dark tobacco wad, juice of which drooled down the corners of his lips. He couldn't take his eyes from the two pointed breasts that stretched this girl's sweater front.

Glenda caught his glare. She'd give him the benefit of the doubt as to his thoughts. However, to save any possible problems which might come up, she moved the button side of her sweater over her breasts. It did little good. The points were still invitingly revealed.

"Where ya from girlie?"

Glenda thought quickly. "Florida."

"Ya mean ya hitch hiked all the way down from

Florida?"

"Yes."

"My—That's a long way, ain't it? What's your name, girlie?"

"Glenda."

"Glenda what? Mine's Charlie Storm."

"Glenda is enough."

"Reckon yer right. I got a farm just a piece up the road. Reckon as how I can't help ya out much more'n fifteen—sixteen miles."

"Every mile counts."

"Goin' far?"

"California."

"My—My. You sure did pick yourself a trip. I been fixin' to hit it West for a long time now. One of these days I'm gonna do just that."

Silence prevailed for several moments then the farmer suddenly pulled his antiquated vehicle off the road and stopped. He flushed slightly as he pulled on the hand brake. "Back tire feels bad— I better take a look," he explained and got out of the car.

He returned a moment later, minus the cud of tobacco he had been chewing. He pulled out a pack of cigarettes from his shirt pocket underneath his overall top. "Want one?"

"No, thank you."

"I do." He lighted up and leaned back in the seat.

"When do we go?"

"You in a hurry, girlie?"

"My name is Glenda."

57

"I like girlie better." He suddenly tossed his cigarette out of the window. "I got all day and you long ago said you was tired of walking." He turned on her. His weather, work beaten hand caught her loose cardigan and pulled her to him. His ugly lips planted themselves firmly on Glenda's; hard; violent. The stink of his breath almost sent her into a swoon, but as if in reflex action her free right hand squared off and slapped him an open palm slap across the face. The man had seemed not to feel the slap. He still held the sweater edge crumpled roughly in his big hand, but he did finally take his lips from hers, however keeping them close to her face.

"You're ruining my sweater. It's the only decent one I have left," she lied, trying for a new approach. Her voice was one of utter pleading.

"Then be good and it won't get hurt," he sneered the remark and threw the sweater edge from his hand. "You got a beautiful mouth. Nice for kissin' and maybe other things. Now make it say the right things to me."

Glenda immediately started to smooth out the injured wool of her sweater. "What do you want?"

For a moment the car rocked with the big man's deep laughter, then he became deadly serious again. "I ain't never met one of you road tramps what ain't always tryin' to make out like the Holiest of Virgins. I bet you been with every road tramp and hobo all the way from Florida. I bet you been with more men than a sinner's got sin. Just because I'm fat, don't make me too heavy to lay with. You'll come around. They all do."

"You can lay yourself and work it anyway you want." Glenda reached for the door handle.

The big farmer's meaty hand reached out quickly and grabbed her by the left breast. Glenda reacted in a scream to the pressure as if the foam rubber he was violently squeezing was actually her flesh. His smile became wicked and the pressure of his hand increased.

"You ain't goin' no place, girlie."

"Let go—you're hurting me."

The man did let go. But not because of her pleading. "Them's the most pretty pair of titties I think I ever did get a feel of. Bet they sure are a pretty sight to see all bare." His big hand slapped the sweater lightly. "Take 'em off."

"Don't be silly."

"I'm tellin' you to start takin' them sweaters off. You either do it by yourself, or I'm doin' it for ya, and I ain't gentle like." He blew his hot, stinking breath into her face. "I swear it. I'll rip that wool till hell won't have it."

Glenda was as frightened as when she had raced out of the Van Carter penthouse. What could she do? She had actually so little choice. But what worried her most was what would happen if she did take the sweater off, then remove her brassiere and this sloppy character's eyes feasted on the breasts that were not there.

"You better get started," he commanded.

Glenda thought fast. She slowly removed her cardigan. She lay it over her lap. She looked toward the man who was now slobbering out of the corner of his mouth. His hand lay at the upper portion of his own leg. He had squirmed in anticipation as the yellow cardigan had come off her body. Glenda turned so that her back was to the man.

"Hey. I don't like fer you to turn around on me like that. I want to see you take off—I like to watch that. I want to see them two things you're so proud of."

Glenda turned her head toward him. "It always embarrasses me to undress in front of a man I'm going to have. I'll turn around in just a second." The sweetness in her voice was all honey.

With her back to him she slowly started to slip the second sweater up over her head. She had to stall for time until some kind of an idea could present itself. Maybe another car would come along. Maybe his passion would subside—but that looked way out of the question. Maybe a lot of things. She so very slowly slipped the sweater up her back, to her neck, up to her hair line.

Charlie's hand shot out and tore the sweater off up over her head. Just as quickly he tossed it on her lap with the cardigan, then with his other hand on her shoulder he spun her around. For the briefest second he caught sight of the pink satin brassiere beneath the matching slip which hid what he wanted to possess. But it was only for a second. Glenda's arms lifted, crisscross, quickly to cover her breasts.

"You sure are lookin' for trouble, girlie," he

muttered. "Now damn it let me see them bare titties you got."

A thought had finally come to her. Now she had a plan of attack. The warm inviting smile captured her features. "I'll give you no trouble at all. I'll even make it easy for you to get. When a man wants something he usually gets it. Especially when the man is as big as you are. Why not lay back and enjoy it."

It hit him right. None of the sex craving left his face but he smiled, friendly now. "Now you're talkin' sense, girlie."

"Please call me Glenda." Her voice was so enticing. She had control now and she knew it but she decided to push it even further. "I'm going to be very nice to you."

"Alright, Glenda . . . But come on. Don't make me wait no more. I got pants somethin' awful— hot as hell." His hand went toward her brassiere which she still covered with her crossed arms.

Glenda pulled back. Still that smile of anticipation. "You don't want to see just my titties, Charlie. Nor just to paw at them without a good finish. You want everything. You want to go all the way. As I said, I'll make it easy for you. You can have me."

The man was startled. "Will you give it to me without no trouble?"

Glenda moved in close. Her arms still covering the brassiere. "Yes," she cooed. "But I want you to see all of me at one time."

"Let's get in the back seat. I got it 'specially

built for such things—cause I'm kinda heavy like." He started to turn toward the door on his side.

"No." She smiled. "It's too confined back there. Let's go where I can give you a good time. When I wiggle you're going to know it and remember it all your life. I have to have lots of room for that. I'm told I'm a good lay; I want you to be able to say it later too." She pointed out her side of the window. "Out in the grass. Behind those bushes over there."

"You're crazy. It's the middle of the winter."

"Only the date tells that. The sun is as warm as if it were summer."

"Well—Okay. I'll get a blanket."

"Don't bother. I like the feeling of the grass on my bare back—and other places—don't you . . . ?"

"Yeah—Yeah—Guess so, never tried before."

"I'll go first and call you when I'm ready."

He turned back on her. A sly look crossed his face. "So once you're outta this car what's to keep you from takin' off down the road?" His eyes narrowed. "I ain't lettin' you run out on me— Not now like when you got me so all fired hot and bothered."

"My suitcase is here in the car and so is my purse. And here. Hold these." She handed him both sweaters. "See. Now how could I run away? Believe me! I want to take care of you—as much as you want me." She paused. "A girl gets hot too, you know."

The man beamed brightly as Glenda got out of

the car and walked to disappear behind some brush several yards off the road. Charlie smiled with anticipation of the ball he would soon be having with this beautiful broad. He sniffed at the sweet perfumed sweater which had so recently encased that beautiful young body—a body he would soon have beneath him—to hold—to caress as he saw fit. And she wasn't going to fight him like others had. He was sure going to have a time of it alright. He put the sweaters carefully in the driver's seat as he shifted his great bulk to the right hand seat. He kept his eyes, now, glued on the brush behind which Glenda had disappeared.

Glenda came out from behind the brush just enough for him to see the lovely body still partially hidden in the tight pink panties and brassiere. Her long auburn hair fell so wonderfully over her white shoulders. Charlie stared out of the car window. Glenda unsnapped the brassiere and turned her back at the same time. With her back to him she let the brassiere fall to the brush. She cupped her hands over her flat boyish nipples feigning full breasts, and turned to him again.

"You can come over now, honey . . ." she cooed.

She again turned her back toward him, slipped out of her panties then dived behind the brush as she heard the car door open.

Charlie had seen her nude back and had seen the panties fall to the ground as she went into the bushes. As he raced the several yards he fumbled at his overall hooks. He reached the bushes. His trousers fell to the ground revealing long underwear. His eyes searched for the beautiful white body of the girl he demanded. The girl whom he had last seen stark naked as she had stepped out of those sheer pink things.

"Honey. Glenda—Where are you?"

"Right here, honey," and it was Glen's deep voice that spoke the words.

All that remained of Glenda was her make-up and wig when Glen stepped out from behind the brush to stand a few feet from the big farmer. Charlie's eyes dropped. His mouth flew open. Glen gave him only a five second look at his nude masculine body, then he slammed a heavy club over the man's left ear. Charlie slumped soundlessly to the ground.

Glen threw the club at the man and stepped back into the brush where he put on Glenda's momentarily discarded clothes.

A moment later Glenda stepped out of the bushes. She went to the fallen man and roughly stripped him of his long underwear and with the overalls she rolled them up in a ball and took them to the car where she threw them on the floor in the front. Then she went back to the fallen man. She stripped off her own panties, urinated in them and threw them across the man's face.

"At least you'll come out of it with the smell of things," laughed Glenda. "Dry them out and maybe you'll get home somehow. You filthy bastard."

Back at the car she found a wallet in the overalls in which was thirty-five dollars. She put the money into her purse, tossed the wallet to the floor and slipped into her sweater set again; arranged the wool over her slacks and got into the car. A moment later the car was chugging along as if nothing had ever stopped it.

Ten miles along the highway she tossed the overalls out onto the cement pavement. The empty wallet followed two miles further on.

CHAPTER ELEVEN

It was a long, almost reckless chance but Glenda took that chance. She drove the old Model "T" a full thousand miles. When it was night and she was so tired that her eyes felt like they would pop their sockets she would stop and sleep in the car. When it was day she continued on, stopping only for gas—a sandwich at roadside stands and to use the "LADIES" room at the gas stations to relieve her kidneys or to shave and rearrange her make-up, then she was on her way again.

Five miles from Lamarr, Colorado, engine smoking like an old steam engine, the old Model "T" gave out. As soon as it had given its last chug, Glenda knew it could never again be repaired. So she let it coast off the highway to the side of the road and applied the quickly failing brakes for the last time.

For several minutes, steam and smoke still pouring from under the hood, she sat with her arms stretched their full length, at the wheel. Her eyes, unseeing, stared straight ahead along the ribbon of highway. Her mind raced back to the present. She sighed and let her arms drop down on her lap. Her slacks had been wrinkled badly from the four days and nights of continuous wearing. She made a face at them and had nearly decided to change into something else when she realized night was falling fast. Why change until morning? Sleep was most important now, besides if she went to sleep after she had changed she'd wake up all wrinkled again. There was no percentage in that.

Glenda was so engrossed in her thoughts that she did not hear the State Police patrol car as it rolled up beside the Model "T." Her head snapped around quickly as the police officer leaned out his window to speak. "Trouble, Miss?"

Glenda looked at them for a long moment. She was certain they could read the horror written across her face.

"No need to be frightened, Miss. We're police officers."

"Yes—Yes—I can see." She started for a smile. "No! No trouble." Again there wasn't the slightest trace of Glen about her voice. It was low and musical. As natural as if it had always been with her. It was so wonderfully smooth it caused her to smile. To smile the smile that had brought so many men to their knees before her.

The officer felt a twinge along his spine. A feeling of utter satisfaction. He felt he was looking at a woman who was as near perfection as any woman could be. She was so luscious it was almost impossible she was "for real."

"No trouble? Your hood looks like a steam engine."

"That's the trouble with old cars," said the second officer. "Come far?"

"Yes. Very far." She indicated the smoking hood. "Just a little overheated. It'll cool off soon."

"We're going through Lamarr. Give you a lift if you want. Sleep in a hotel and pick up the car tomorrow."

It would be the height of her ambition to ride the five miles dressed as a girl in that patrol car with two policemen and never be detected. But even as she thought it, she realized this was neither the time or place for such an adventure. She had been driving a hot car and Glen, her counterpart, was wanted for murder. Sooner or later recognition could come, especially if Glenda was unmasked.

"No thanks. Old jenny here will be alright in a few minutes." She sighed. "I want to be a long way the other side of Lamarr by midnight."

"Okay. But watch yourself. Don't pick up any hitch hikers. Had a lot of dangerous ones through here this month."

"I never pick up anyone." She had almost sounded insulted.

The policeman turned to the driver. "Let's go Mac."

Mac leaned over his partner to take a good look at the girl. His face was stern. "I think we oughta figure out some thing where by we can take her in and lock her up for a spell."

Glenda pulled back startled.

"Why?" The partner was serious.

"So's we have her for the policeman's picnic next week. She's the prettiest thing I've seen around these parts for years."

Both the officers burst out with heavy laughter as Mac put the car into motion.

Glenda let her breath go out in an explosive

sigh of relief only when she could no longer see the police car on the road ahead. As soon as she could regain any composure at all she quickly opened her suitcase and began to remove her make-up.

* * * *

Glen, dressed in his neatly pressed gray suit and blue suede shoes, packed the beige slacks, wig and yellow sweater set along with Glenda's other feminine things into the suitcase on top of the fur jacket, then secured the lock and strap. He looked both ways on the road to make sure the police car was nowhere in sight, then he got out of the car and began to walk along the highway in the direction of Lamarr, five miles away. Glen and Glenda would sleep in a hotel, or motel, this night, even if it would take an hour or more to walk that five miles.

CHAPTER TWELVE

Glen parked his bags in a room at the best of Lamarr, Colorado's three hotels, then intent on finding a bar and having several good drinks, he walked out into the town's cool night air. For one thing he felt he rated a couple of drinks and second they would fortify his thinking to a clearer channel and then too he hadn't had a drink since that night at Dalten Van Carter's penthouse over a week before.

The bar he chose was one of extremely unstable character. Its occupants looked like the cast of characters in a cheap western motion picture saloon, minus their guns and holsters. All wore the ranch garb, big hats and well worn high heeled boots. Even though he felt strongly out of place in this atmosphere, Glen moved up to stand at the bar. The barkeep that moved up to take his order was indeed to say the least, a rugged looking individual. Glen had seen a lot of pug-uglies at ring side in his short twenty-six years, but this guy had them all beat. His voice was stone gravel.

"What da ya want?"

"Martini."

"A real fancy dude, huh?" He was shouting his words more to the crowded saloon than to Glen. "He wants a Martini."

The mob laughed and a few remarks were thrown, which made Glen both mad and nervous, but nothing further happened. The bartender leaned across so that his face was but inches from Glen's. The pug-ugly features broke out into a wide grin. "Don't mind me fella. I'm always joshin' with the boys. I'm Happy Chandler. I own this joint. You bein' a new comer wouldn't know that. Anyway. We don't make no mixed drinks in here. Only place what does is the Packard Hotel down the street. The boys here are all hard working ranch hands what takes 'em straight or with beer chasers. Some only drinks beer. I ken scare up some coke or ginger ale fer chasers iffin' ya wants." Then he pulled back.

Glen was glad to be rid of Pug-Ugly. The man's breath had smelled like stale potatoes mixed with garlic; it also made Glenda remember another incident, back along the road.

"Whiskey and water on the side," said Glen with a slight trace of Glenda's tone in the voice.

Pug-Ugly, Happy Chandler, did a double take then snapped his hand to his cauliflower ear. He was sure the sound he heard came from within his own head. He'd have to see a doctor about those ringing noises one of these days. Then he moved to get the drink. Glen made a mental note that not only did Glenda have to watch Glen's voice, but Glen most certainly had to be careful of Glenda's musical tones.

Glen was reading a carnival notice on a billboard behind the counter when Pug-Ugly brought his drink and set it in front of him. The ugly man's eyes went to the carnival notice then back to Glen. "Comes in tomorrow morning. Always did like the carnival. This is the first one this season. Ought to make out real good if the weather holds for it. The boys got their season's pay this past week."

The two policemen entered quickly. One stayed at the door while the other went to the far end of the bar. Pug-Ugly, Happy Chandler, leaned across the bar to yell at the policeman who had remained stationed at the door.

"What's up, Mac?"

"Nothing to worry you, Happy."

"Lookin' fer somebody special?"

"Could be."

Glen buried his face in his drink. The second cop was looking at each of the saloon's inmates. Some he knew and accepted and returned their greeting during his slow walk along the length of the bar, back toward the door. Twice he stopped to check the identification of people. One of which looked too young to be in the bar and drinking, but it must have been in order because the cop handed him back the identification card and continued on. The cop took a quick look around again then moved up to an old bum at the bar. The bum could produce no identification so the cop took him by the arm and slapped a handcuff to his wrist. The old bum reached out with his still free hand to grip his big glass of beer which he slugged down; replaced the glass to the bar then followed the officer as if this were an every day occurrence for him.

The traversing policeman handed the bum over to the cop at the door then turned to look again into the saloon's interior. His eyes stopped on Glen. He quickly sized up the well dressed young man then walked over to him. He put his hand lightly on Glen's shoulder. Glen turned to him. It was the policeman from the state patrol car which had stopped to be of assistance to Glenda earlier. There was no menace in the policeman's face or voice as he spoke.

"Do I know you from someplace?"

"I'm sure you don't officer." Glen had to be polite.

"Your face sure looks familiar."

"I've never been in Lamarr before. Only arrived here this afternoon." Glen had to control Glenda's tone now for sure. This policeman would surely recognize the similarity, or had he seen a wanted poster with Glen's picture and it wouldn't come into focus in his mind? The Carnival notice caught the corner of Glen's eye. "I'm with the carnival coming in tomorrow. My first season out with it. I'm staying the night up at the hotel. The Grandview."

The cop fingered the material of Glen's lapel. "You're sure better dressed than most Carneys I've ever seen."

Glen laughed. Oh-oh—Too musical. He looked serious again. "Guess I've still got most of my self respect left." Glen smiled. "Like I said. It's my first season out."

It didn't convince the cop as it should have. "You got some identification?"

"Sure!" Glen's hand started slowly for his wallet

in his rear pocket. A cold fear going through his body with every muscle movement. What if the cop recognized the name.

"Ahh, come on Ernie. Stop layin' it to my customers. He's alright." Pug-Ugly was serious.

"Yeah, Ernie. He's right. We got orders these carney guys ain't to be bothered this year unless they ask for it." The cop at the door was also serious.

Ernie, the cop, turned away to join his partner. He turned back to look at Glen. "Keep your nose clean while you're in this town." He turned back to his partner. "We'd better take old Henry in before his wife gets on the department again." At the door he again turned to face Glen. "I'll be out at the carney grounds tomorrow night. What show did you say you worked?"

Glen thought fast. "I didn't say."

"Guess that's right. Well? What show are you with?"

"I'm a barker." It was the first thing that jumped into his mind.

The cop laughed. "Good. Old friends and the police can still get in free, can't they?"

"Try and stop them . . ." Pug-Ugly chirped in.

Ernie was still laughing as Mac drove the patrol car off along Lamarr's main business street, siren suddenly bursting into action.

Pug-Ugly, Happy Chandler, moved in close to Glen. "They pick old Henry up every time he gets out. His wife gives him a bad time and when he finally escapes she gives the department a bad

74

time—so they pick him up."

"Why the siren?"

"Old Henry likes to hear it. Them too! His wife knows he's been picked up, and she comes to get him. Bout the only time the boys ever get to use the siren now-a-days." He smiled. "Don't mind the boys askin' all them questions. They got a job to do. Had a lot of characters comin' through town lately. Two of them was murderers before they left town; a third became a murderer just outside of town. Killed an old lady who was givin' him a hand out. Caught up with him around Pueblo. So the boys are on their toes about anybody new in town they don't know."

"Like you said. They have their job to do." Glen felt he could get to like Pug-Ugly, if only his breath wasn't so bad.

"Both Ernie and Mac are a coupla good joes. Just treat 'em right, that's all."

"That's fine," said Glen. Why should he care.

Glen, however, began to realize one thing. This time he had really put his foot into it. It wasn't going to be easy for him to leave town unless it was with the carnival.

CHAPTER THIRTEEN

The bartender remained at the far end of his bar for a long time after the two cops had gone; almost as if he expected their momentary return. But after that breathing time he made his way back to where Glen was seated sipping his drink.

"Want another one?" Pug-Ugly seemed to be trying to feel his way into further conversation, then added, "On the house."

"Sure—Why not?"

Pug-Ugly remained silent as he got the drinks. He spoke again when he sat the whiskey drink down in front of Glen and drew a beer for himself.

"Lots of road tramps thumbing through here these days." He took a big, sloppy gulp of the beer. "Some get around to causin' Mac and Ernie a lot of trouble."

"Do I look like a road tramp?"

"Ain't like the old days. Ain't many do look the part. See! We got a 'Green River' law down here."

"What in the world is a 'Green River' law?"

"A kinda law that keeps them door to door sales guys off our backs. They hit this town like a swarm of locust a few years back. Made deals on a lot of things; magazines; pills; face soap that takes out wrinkles; miracle seeds; any kind of gimmick thing. Sure! They make their deal; pick up a quick advance in cash; give out with a phony receipt and then they're gone. Nobody sees them, the cash and most of all the folks never see what they bought. Course—Lots of them sales folks is honest hard working citizens. But because of the bad ones, everybody's gotta suffer."

"I don't like being bugged—by cops or anyone else."

"Sure—Sure—but take my advice. Don't mess with Mac and Ernie. Like I say. They can get pretty riled up if they have a mind to—and the law is on their side. They are the law!" This last was hard, definite, pointed.

"Those two are your police force?"

"Naw. We got a sheriff and two deputies for the town. They don't 'mount to much. Usually find them over at Clem's General Store playin' penny-ante poker. Nope! Mac and Ernie are State Patrol boys—they're the real town law. They run this town. Like I say. Maybe they get hard at times. But they got reason. Besides. Again like I say. Town's gotta have some law—'stead of penny-ante poker players. Mac and Ernie sure run this town alright." Pug-Ugly paused only long enough to pour himself another glass of tap beer. "You stayin' long?"

"How long is the carnival staying?"

"Usually a week! Don't you know?"

"I only run the concessions. The owners don't tell me much. I set up—let the folks play out the game—then move on when and where they tell me."

"You got a good game?"

"When I have a game going."

"I'm closing up early tomorrow. I expect I'll come on out to the fair grounds."

"You just do that—Be glad to see you."

"That's all?"

"I don't get you?"

"You are new at the game, aren't you?" He laughed. "Look. Usually the carney fellas give me a break—Like I give 'em a free drink now and again." Pug-Ugly indicated the glass in front of Glen as he finished his words.

"Sure—Sure—You just look me up. I'll see you get a break."

"Say. That's mighty white of you." The bartender gulped down his beer in one quick slug. "Where do I find you?"

"Look around. I'll be there."

"But what game?"

"Who knows?"

"You don't even know what game you'll be at?"

"As I told the cops. I'm only a concessionaire. I never know what tent the boss will put me under. Might even be the snake show."

"I hope not?"

"Why? "

"I can think of lots better things I'd rather watch wiggle than a bunch of snakes—Say— You're a strange kid for a barker."

"How so?"

"You ain't got one of them crazy voices like most of them has. You know. Husky soundin'?"

"I studied voice and acting once."

"Reckon that accounts for it. You got a car?"

"I came in by bus. I'd planned to rent one tomorrow."

"Fair grounds a long way from here. How you gonna get out there?"

"If I go out tonight I suppose I'll need a cab."

"Sure you will—You don't want to stay at the hotel."

"I'm already registered."

"It's a flea bag."

"Is a carnival tent any better?"

"How should I know—Oh, I get it. Anyway. That's old Ezra Ballis over there on the corner. He's a taxi of sorts. When him and his heap can make it. He's asleep now but I'll wake him when you're ready to go. You want another?"

"Why not?"

The bartender became silent again until after he had mixed the drink and set it in front of Glen. "Dollar and two bits . . ."

"For one drink? I thought you bought me the last beer."

Glen reached into his pocket and produced two one dollar bills which he laid on the bar. "Have another then."

"Using your words—Don't mind if I do."

The bartender drew another tap beer.

CHAPTER FOURTEEN

Glen pulled his lapels up against a slight drizzle as he stepped out of the saloon followed by the ancient cabbie who led him quickly to as equally an ancient vehicle parked at the curb.

"Hotel ain't far," muttered the old man getting in behind the wheel and slamming the door behind him.

Glen, left behind, shrugged then got into the rear seat. "I know. I'd walk but I don't like walking in the rain."

The old man started his chatter almost before he had hit the car starter. "You oughta get out to a motel near the fair grounds. Be closer if you're one of them carney folks."

"I've got a room at the hotel."

"Huh?"

"The hotel." He said it loud.

"You're the boss."

The old car moved forward.

Glen's mind wandered. He spoke silently to himself as he looked out of the window and watched the increasing rain. "A good night's rest is just what the doctor would order." He paused in his own thinking. "Glenda needs it more than I do—Glenda!" A realization came over him suddenly. He didn't have a nightgown in his bag. Glenda never slept nude and just didn't appreciate using a slip for such night wear. Without a proper nightgown Glenda would roll and toss all night in the desire for one.

"Are there any shops open?" he finally said.

The old man shook his head. "They all closes up 'roun' six o'clock."

"Nothing at all open?"

"What ya want to get?"

"None of your business."

"That way, huh?"

"That way!"

"Can't help ya much if I don't know what ya wants."

"Let's say—I need some clean shorts."

"Unnerwear, huh?"

"Yes."

"Well—We got one of them new-fangled Cut-Rate Drug Super Market places out on the edge of town. They sell most anything 'ceptin' medicine I reckon. Even see'd some shoes out there— last time I was out that way."

"Go out there."

"Sure." He spoke slyly then. "Cost you a buck an' a half."

"I can pay."

"Cost you another half buck for me to wait on ya while ya shops."

"I think I can scrape it together."

"Sure ya could." The old cabbie ducked his head slightly so as to permit him to look skyward. The rain was falling harder. "Maybe ya best look inta getting yerself a rain coat—This one's gonna last awhile. Maybe a coupla days. Not so good fer yer carney, huh?"

"Guess not." Glen was very unconcerned about

the Carnival at that moment. Only the night-gown was foremost in his mind. Glenda was taking over fast. Glenda was taking over more and more. He'd have to watch that very closely.

They had past the city lights and had entered a stretch of darkness, then just ahead of them the bright lights of a Cut Rate Drug Store-Supermarket combination cut through the heavy rain. The cabbie cut his wheels so that he turned his taxi off the main road and entered into the large parking area. He came to a stop near the drug store entrance. "I'll be right out," said Glen.

"Take yer time—ain't no extra charge—'ception what I told ya."

Glen got out of the cab and made his way the few steps to the store and entered.

He was pleased to see the store was nearly void of patrons so he selected a pleasant looking elderly saleslady in a white smock and moved to her.

"Are you busy ma'am?"

"Not at all young man."

"My wife and I are at the hotel in town."

"Yes?" The woman had a pleasant smile.

"She needs a nightgown. Would you have such a thing?"

"Nothing very exciting or expensive—The dress shop in town would be the only place for anything like that."

"I'm sure anything you have will be fine for the night." He spoke, perhaps, a little too insistently.

"Follow me, please."

She led him through a maze of counters to one

holding several selections of the cheaper varieties of nylon and cotton panties, brassieres, and an even smaller selection of nightgowns.

"Any special material?"

"Anything but cotton." Again there was a bit too much insistence.

"What size?"

"Fourteen."

"Hum, hum," she mused, then fondled through several of the garments to finally come up with a pink rayon stripe affair. "There—just the right size." She had turned to hold it up almost as if she were sizing it to him, but a foot or two away from his actual frame. "Two ninety-eight," she finally said.

"Yes—that will do fine—and I think I'd better have a pair of slippers also—size eight."

"With or without heels?"

"At least two inch heels."

She moved on to another counter. She browsed through a pile of slippers and then turned to hand him a set of slippers made of a light pink plastic.

"There."

"Those will be fine." Glenda was feeling better already. Glen's eyes might betray her. "How much?"

"Two ninety-eight for the gown, one forty-five for the slippers—thirty cents tax—Four seventy-three." Then she quickly said, "We have a floor length housecoat—you might call it a negligee, that will match the gown. It's marked down to three ninety-eight."

Glen had nearly forgotten. For a moment his mind drifted back to thoughts of the marabous, the satin and nylon negligees that were lost forever back in his apartment, so very far away.

"Yes. That is a thought." He quickly added, "Same size."

The woman, wise beyond her appearance, said, "Yes, I know," and she moved off along the counters. Glen thought he had caught the faintest glimpse of a smile trailing along the edges of her lips.

A moment later the saleslady returned with a wrap around rayon strip negligee. "Nine dollars even," she smiled at him.

Glen paid the woman, accepted his change and the package then turned to go. "Wear them in good health." Her voice cut through him. He stopped; turned toward her again. She smiled knowingly.

Glen paused a moment more then turned away again. Somewhere along the way he had let Glenda slip through almost completely.

CHAPTER FIFTEEN

Glen awoke first at eight o'clock, but the muggy rain drenched day caused him to turn his head away from the unshaded window, pull down the nightgown which had crept up around his middle during the night; made a mental note to get some better ones later in the day, then went back to sleep again.

It was close to noon before he awoke ready at last for the day. He leaned back against the pillows, hands behind his head, for a long moment and stretched strongly before he reached for a cigarette. Taking each inhalation quickly and deeply he finished the life of the cigarette in far shorter time than its usual burning time. After snuffing the butt out in the bedside ash tray he pushed back the covers, swung his feet free to snuggle into the slippers, and eased on the rayon stripe negligee. He tied it securely around the middle then made his way to the bathroom.

"Damn," he muttered. "No shower. I didn't notice it last night. Guess Pug-Ugly was right. It is a flea bag."

He studied his face in the mirror for a long moment and decided as soon as he shaved he would have to pluck his eyebrows again, then he drew a bath.

'Glen had stopped in town where he bought an inexpensive used Buick convertible. He paid cash for the new car and registered it in the name of Glen Starr. Next he drove to one of the three dress shops in town and purchased several expensive nightgowns, a pink quilted satin bed jacket and a blue quilted nylon floor length housecoat. With the packages securely locked in the trunk of his car he drove back in the direction of the town and the fair grounds beyond.

It was two-thirty by the time Glen parked near the entrance gate which, as most of the carnival itself, was still under construction. He moved to one of the Roust-A-Bouts who was busily banging a giant iron spike into the ground.

"Who owns this show?" asked Glen pleasantly.

Without looking up or missing a stroke with his spike hammer, the man indicated the sign above the gate he was constructing. Glen looked up. The sign read:

J.M. GREATER'S GREATER SHOW
ATTRACTIONS

Glen looked back to the man. "Where do I find J.M. Greater?"

"In a grave yard—Sioux City I think. He's dead some fifteen years." The man began to laugh stupidly at his own idea of a joke.

Glen became immediately annoyed at the man's apparent ignorance and attitude. "So who is in charge?"

"Bill Greater. The old man's son."

Glen's eyes began to show the violence that was building inside him. Had he a gun at that moment there would be one less Roust-A-Bout in the world. The Roust-A-Bout seemed to sense a danger his small mind might not be able to cope with. It was not an intelligent sense, but more of an animal sense. The Roust-A-Bout stopped his work, rubbed the drying rain from his forehead and looked directly at Glen. "You'll probably find him in the office." He pointed to a trailer behind the "Snake Show."

"That there trailer."

Glen didn't neglect to thank the man—he just ignored the courtesy as he turned away and walked to the trailer.

A hefty voice called, "Come in," to Glen's insistent knocking.

Glen opened the door and entered to find a rather shabbily furnished trailer and an equally as shabby a man. Bill Greater was a man in his late fifties. He wore clean but creaseless trousers of gray wool and a brown wool shirt topped with a fancy yellow vest. To top off his incongruous outfit he wore black and white shoes and a brown bowler hat. A dead cigar stub occupied the corner of his thick lips. "What'd ya want?" He paused then snapped his eyes menacingly at Glen. "You a bill collector?"

"No—I'm not a bill collector."

"Ohh—I get it." He took a roll of bills from his pocket. "You're from the city boys. Okay! How much more is the shake down?"

"Put your money away!"

Bill Greater was shocked for a minute. "Not from the city, huh?"

Glen nodded his head.

Then Bill Greater thought he had it. His face went into a scowl. "Beat it bum—I ain't got no jobs for no drifters—unless you're a Roust-A-Bout or a Geek and you don't look big enough to be a Roust-A-Bout or drunk enough to be a Geek."

"It isn't a job I want from you either."

"Damn it all to hell—What in hell do you want from me?" Mr. Greater was becoming even more exasperated.

"Any of your shows or concessions want to sell out?"

"Sell—my boys?"

"Yeah!"

Bill Greater's mind flashed back to the four solid weeks of rain outs he had just suffered through and this spot looked like it would match the others. He had loaned cash to nearly every show owner and concessionaire on the lot. They were into him for plenty and he held mortgages on most of them. They'd sell if he said so. Why should he take the losses, especially when here in front of him was a real live sucker. Bill Greater had learned long ago that a sucker is a sucker and he'd better strike while the mark was hot. But not too fast. Never sell too fast. "My boys are all happy with me," he finally said.

"Sure they are—but who wants out?"

This guy wasn't going to be an easy mark but he'd handled a lot of tough ones in his time. "What kinda show you got in mind, stranger?"

Bill Greater was calm—conniving.

"Maybe the girlie show—Maybe the side show—What have you got going?"

"Them's big operations."

"Your whole layout is about the smallest operation I've ever come across."

"You're a carney man?"

"What's that matter! I know a small layout when I see one."

That did it. Bill Greater burned. "Maybe you think you'd like to take over the whole show?"

"Maybe I would at that," Glen spit back quickly.

Bill Greater's mind clicked fast. The whole shebang wasn't worth five thousand bucks. It had been a bad season all the way. The insurance company wouldn't renew his insurance on several of the rides because of their condition and he wasn't about to throw good money after bad by fixing them up. Only way the officials in any town let him get away with setting those certain rides up was because when asked about insurance he showed his blanket policies which in small print stated the rides were not included but who ever reads the small print. At the top of the pages were the letters spelling out a big company name and the words INSURANCE and the current dates. That's all they needed to know. Top of that— another week of rain, half his "boys" would leave him, those that still owned their own shows or concessions anyway and that would leave him with practically no show at all. He certainly couldn't afford to pay somebody to run the other shows even if he took them over. In another week the traveling expenses would present themselves again. How could he arrange that. He couldn't carry these lugs any longer yet he didn't have any show without them. Four weeks it had been one hundred percent out go; before that; very little better and this week promised more of the same. The show wasn't worth five thousand dollars—the amount it would take to keep going for another month.

"Ten grand," he finally said.

"For what?"

"The whole operation."

"Ten grand for this flea bag?"

Bill Greater knew his whole operation was a "Rag-Bag" but he wasn't going to recoup his losses in any other way. Sell out—that's the only way he'd have enough to form up again next season and maybe have better luck. "There's a lot of good stock here, mister."

"It's falling apart."

"Then why do you want it?"

"Maybe I like carnivals—Maybe I can make something out of it."

"Eight thousand."

"Seventy-five hundred," Glen countered his offer.

"Eight thousand and not a penny less."

"Eight thousand it is."

"You're buying?" Bill Greater was indeed surprised.

"At that last price."

"Cash?"

"Cash!"

Bill Greater stood up with a hastily out-stretched hand. "Mister. You got yourself a carnival."

Glen ignored his hand. "Get out your papers."

"Got 'em all right here." He turned to the desk and pulled out several papers.

Glen counted out the money and put it in front of Bill Greater. "This trailer goes with the deal."

Indignantly. "My home?"

"That's the deal."

Bill Greater shrugged, signed the papers; pocketed the cash then turned to Glen. Glen signed next as the big man pulled another paper out of his desk and handed it in an envelope to him.

"The insurance papers," replied Bill Greater by way of an explanation.

CHAPTER SIXTEEN

From the bare ground to the finished product the carnival was hastily assembled. The husky Roust-A-Bouts, doing most of the manual, building, labor made almost a musical dirge with their great hammers; their slashing saws; the squeak of bent nails being removed.

Planks. Fresh lumber. Steel rods slammed to the ground and awaited usage. Trucks were hastily unloaded; the material almost immediately being carted away. Ground was broken. Frames began to take shape. Tents were unrolled; center poles were shoved underneath for the raising. The ropes became secured. Iron and steel took the form of various rides. Circus type wagons took their places behind the tents. Flats and boards took the shape of ticket booths in front of the steadily shape taking rides and shows. Banners began to appear over the entrance of the girlie show; the snake show; the western show; the Hawaiian show. Wheels and spinners snapped into place in the concession booths. Multicolored counters seemed to jump into position. Plaster dolls; trophies and other 'schluck' materials were wrapped or unwrapped and placed on shelves in an alluring manner.

Then the layout of all the tent shows sprouted to finishing touches as the long Side Show banner was tied into place. The great banner boasted gigantic cartoons of what was to be formed on the inside. The Fat Lady. The Tattooed Woman. The

Indian Rubber Man. A Hindu spread out on nails. The Fire Eater; and an extra large poster of the Half-Man, Half-Woman, blow off attraction.

Noises of every description resounded throughout the entire area and it was into this fantastic scene Glen walked from his new office.

His eyes marveled at the speed and accuracy with which the work was accomplished. Each man knowing his job and doing it with the precision only experience could teach.

Glen walked around 'his' growing carnival a long time until he came to the Side Show. There the fantastic poster of the Half-Man, Half-Woman caused him to come to a dead stop. His eyes seemed to refuse leaving the cartoon. Immediately he knew he must meet this one. He had started for the rear of the tent, the trailer living quarters, when the voice stopped him.

"Told you we'd be dropping by."

Glen knew who the voice belonged to even before he turned.

Ernie, the cop, was behind the steering wheel of his state patrol car and Mac was beside him. Glen moved to the car.

"You're early. Nothing opens until seven."

Ernie continued staring at Glen which made Glen nervous, but when the cop spoke he directed his words to his partner Mac.

"Like we ain't never been on a carney lot before, Mac." Then the big cop directed his voice to Glen. "You workin' the side show this trip?"

"What's it look like?"

"Where's Greater?"

"Gone."

"How's that?"

"He doesn't own J.M. Greater's Greater Show Attractions any longer."

Ernie and Mac glanced quickly at each other. Ernie then snapped to Glen. "Who pays the bills?"

"I do."

Again the two cops looked briefly at each other before Mac leaned over to speak again.

"Comin' up in the world, huh?"

"I know a good deal when I see it."

"Where's a punk like you get cash for a carney this size?"

"I saved my money. Besides it's a Rag-Bag. I got it cheap."

"You pay the bills, huh?"

"That's what I said." Glen was steaming, but he held his temper as he said, "How much?"

Ernie turned to face Mac directly this time. "Now what ever does he mean?" He snapped back to Glen. "Greater pays off. You hear?"

"He told me he already had paid off."

"Maybe to the city boys. You're over the city line. This is our territory."

"You?"

Ernie came out of the patrol car and slammed the door behind him. Mac mirrored his movements on the other side, but did not leave his door. After he had closed it, he leaned up against the fender, his arms on the hood.

"Ernie's gonna get mad—speakin' out loud like that around where there's lots of ears—Sir!" Then he took out a cigar and lit it.

Ernie had looked to him during his words, then turned slowly back to Glen. His words came just as slowly. "This is the way it's gonna be buster." He grabbed Glen by the arm. "Let's go downtown, buster."

Glen was frightened but he didn't admit this fact to the cop's face nor did he permit it to show on his own features. He forced a heavy shrug of his shoulders which loosened the cop's hand. "Let's keep your hands off me. That is unless you have something to charge me with and you'd better make sure the charge will stick if you do roust me. Just keep your hands off me."

Mac came around the car fast. He moved in close to Glen's face. "This is the way it's gonna be buster." He grabbed Glen by the lapels, pulled him in close to his, then he whispered in Glen's ear; hard but still a whisper; venom, but still a whisper. "One hundred a night for each of us. That's two hundred a night. One for each of us. Me and my partner. Every night of the week your outfit is here. Call it rent. Call it anything you want. It's two hundred all the same."

Mac let go of Glen's lapels, pushing him backward at the same time. "You're open, according to your permit, until two A.M.—We collect at midnight—every night—every night—midnight."

Ernie moved in beside Mac. "See you at midnight, sir."

Mac moved back to enter his side of the patrol car. Ernie indignantly flipped Glen's tie from his suit, then slid in behind the steering wheel.

The state patrol car moved off down the midway in a rush of dirt and mud.

Without thinking Glen shouted. "And I don't allow outside cars on my mid-way." It, however, had come out in *Glenda's* full round tones.

"Cops never like to be shouted at, dearie." An almost feminine voice. One he had not heard before.

Glen spun back to the nearly completed side show tent. She was dressed in a pair of well used velvet Capri and long sleeved white satin blouse. Her face implacably made up with deep red lipstick, eye shading and rouge. Glen was amazed to see one side of her hair was cut in boy-like style, while the other was long and fell in curls down over her shoulders; as blonde as a dye pot could make it.

Glen moved to her.

CHAPTER SEVENTEEN

Glen looked to the pointed scarlet painted nails on her long slender fingers as the girl held out her hand daintily. "You must be the new owner?" she said.

Glen took her hand. "My," the girl noted quickly. "Your nails are nearly as long as mine. Pretty! Pretty! Come on back to my trailer. We can have a drink from my private bottle and get better acquainted."

And as from the moment she started she didn't wait for Glen's answer. She hooked her arm around his and led him off through the Side Show tent to a small trailer in the rear.

"Come on in. It's small but comfortable." Immediately she disappeared inside. Glen followed shortly after.

She had been telling the truth. It was small, but comfortable. A soft sofa-bed. A small alcohol stove. A midget refrigerator and a dressing screen which had two fluffy negligees and a pair of nylon stockings hanging over it.

"Sit down. Make yourself at home. I'll get us a stiff one. I'm already a half pint or more up on you."

Glen lowered his frame onto the sofa bed as the girl went about pouring drinks and backing them up with ice water.

"Hope you like it with ice water. It's the only mix I have." She crossed to him; handed him the drink then curled up on the sofa-bed beside him.

"You're cute for a boss. Drink alright?"

Glen finally got a word in. "It's fine."

"I'm the half and half. Half man, half woman act, you know. The blow off for the Side Show. 1 give the suckers a long pitch, sell them some photographs of me and get them out. I prefer being called Shirlee—with two E's. I suppose I did have a name like Robert or Andrew or Tom on my birth certificate—it's been so long since I've seen it, I can't remember for sure just what it was. What's yours?"

"Glen."

"Oh, come now, dearie—I heard that voice when she screamed at the fuzz a little bit ago." Shirlee lit a cigarette and talked through the smoke as it drifted up around her head. "You know the old saying—It takes one to know one. Come on, honey, tell Auntie Shirlee all about it. What's a nice lookin' one like you buyin' a flea-circus like this for. With your looks you could be making it big in the big town." Then she got an idea. She took both their glasses and proceeded across the trailer to the bottle where she refilled them. "Then maybe you've already hit the big time. Where'd one of your tender years get enough cash to buy such an outfit as this? Ah, yes. That's what the cop asked you! Little matter! I'm not one to pry into other people's personal lives." She returned with the refilled glasses; again one of which she handed to Glen.

Glen, puzzled by this *girl's* open frankness and continual run of words, took a great gulp of the hot liquor. Shirlee sunk down beside him on the sofa-bed again.

"You ever work in *drag*, dearie?" she continued.

This sudden question caused Glen to cast his eyes downward in an embarrassed glance.

"You don't have to answer that! It's written all over you. The thinly plucked eyebrows. Those beautiful long fingernails. One looks closely enough they can still see traces of polish near the cuticles." Glen snapped a look to his own fingernails at this as the girl continued. "Where'd you work, honey? The clubs?"

"Yes, the clubs." Glen said it so slowly.

"I thought so. Can't fool an old Pro like me, dearie. I've been a female impersonator a good many years. Ohh, I'm a lot older than I look. The face paint takes care of that—and good hot steam baths. Would you believe it—I'm well into my thirties. I worked the clubs for a long time. Washington, San Francisco, the Village in New York. Even Los Angeles before the cops closed up all the gay joint shows. Used to have a hell of a good one on La Brea Avenue out there in Hollywood. Three months I tried to get in that spot. Twenty or more auditions. Then when I finally land the job they close the club on my opening night. I like the carnival because I live as I want— all the time just as I want.

Shirlee had finished her drink. She glanced to Glen's glass and saw it was still half full. She got up, refilled her own glass and returned.

"My you're a quiet one," she said as she sunk

down to the sofa-bed again. "I'd planned to wash my hair and set it this afternoon, but you've taken up so much of my time I suppose I'll have to do it tomorrow. I like rubber. Did you ever use rubber, honey? Head to foot I mean? You oughta try it sometime." She went into a sex thought of ecstasy. "Ohh, the smell of it. The confining feeling . . ." She gulped down a great portion of her drink. She calmed her speeding urges; breathed heavily several times, then with sheepish eyes looked up to Glen again. "I'm sorry." She took another slug from her glass. "I get carried away sometimes when I think of the things which inspire my sex life." She slugged down the remainder of her drink and just as quickly had gone to the bottle and refilled the glass. However, this time when she returned she folded into a large easy chair next to the sofa-bed. "Didn't offer you one 'cause you still got some. When you want a refill just holler out." She crushed her cigarette out on the floor with a grind of her toe. Glen made a mental note that this practice would cease. One miss of her toe on those lighted coals and the whole show could go up in smoke.

Shirlee's voice became whiskey thick. "Meet old Doc Henry yet?"

This time she waited for an answer. Glen slowly spoke. "No, I haven't."

"You will. But even as young as you are—you're too old for him. He likes young boys. Ten. Twelve. Thirteen. He's a son of a bitchin' bastard creep. You ain't gonna find anybody around here that likes that son of a bitchin' creep. It's his son of a bitchin' creep kind that makes a bad name for everybody who is a—little—different." She became hard. "I hate him. I hate him worse'n poison. I hate that son of a bitchin' bastard. Somebody oughta cut his nuts off. Even that'd be too good for him."

"I think I'd better go now." Glen stood up.

"You don't like me."

"I like you fine." Glen finished his drink. "Shall I get rid of this Doc Henry?"

"You do and I'll cut your heart out and feed it to the snakes." Her voice was hard with venom.

"I thought you didn't like him?"

"I hate the son of a bitchin' bastard." She snapped out of her chair, slopped more whiskey into her glass and slugged it down; slopped in another glass full. "You like to drink, dearie?" She slugged that one down too and again refilled the glass. "I do. It's kinda a glow you don't get from nothin' else and I ain't one of them bastard creeps that takes dope." Suddenly Shirlee remembered a point which had not been completed. "You don't get rid of old Doc. He's the best toe man in the business. He sure is good with the toes. Gets his kicks that way. He can chew on a toe better'n anybody you ever heard of. You ever had some-body chew on your toes? Ha? Maybe you did but you ain't the type to admit it. Want to know why I let him chew on my toes? Because I like it. I like it better if I got rubber boots on—real thin rubber so you can feel your toes through it yet you know it's there. You shouldn't oughta shout at cops with your other voice. Might give you a peck of trouble. And be careful of that Tillie. The Tattooed Woman. She's no good. A real trouble maker. Woman! She ain't no more of a woman than me. She hides the same thing in her panties as I do and not as good either." Shirlee paused again only long enough to slug down her drink and pour another; the last in the bottle.

Shirlee studied the empty then threw the 'dead soldier' into a bucket across the room. She turned to the door; threw it open and shouted, "Terrible—Terrible—Come over here you Indian Apache renegade. Get over here and I mean right now."

A string-bean type elderly Indian in dirty clothes appeared in the doorway. "Terrible come," he muttered through hard eyes.

"You ain't yet, Apache—but take one of my photographs over to the bathroom with you and maybe you will. In the meantime get me a bottle of whiskey and make it fast."

"Si," he said, and the insulted Indian turned away. Shirlee slammed the door behind him.

"Tillie," Shirlee mumbled. "Now there's a trouble makin' creep for you." She sneered. "Tillie the Tattooed Lady. Lady—huh! It's just like I told you. She's got the same thing in her panties as you and I got." Another thought suddenly crossed her features. "You do wear panties, don't you? Of course you do! I do all the time—brassiere too—I couldn't think of putting on those horrible shorts all *men* are supposed to wear. Conventions! huh—You know where they can stick their conventions." She began to pace the small trailer area; back and forth. "Where's that God-damned Apache with my whiskey?" A deep thought furrowed her brow. "Must be somebody around this fire trap I like—only I ain't found one yet. Maybe I'll like you. Maybe I won't. If I don' I'll take off—cut right out of here. I don't stay where I don't like to stay. Maybe I could get back in the clubs again. Make some real money for a change. Said I drink too much. Huh! Just because I missed a couple of shows . . ." Shirlee suddenly began laughing. She turned on Glen and babbled thickly through her laughter. "One night I took a dive off the stage and landed right in the middle of a table, right on top of some real broad type girl. Tore her dress right down the middle and there were two big titties starin' me right in the eyes—a real bust in the eye—get it—and—and the broad's escort with his eyes bulging out like he'd never seen them before. What a spill that was." The laugh ceased and she became drunkenly serious again. "Closed the club—spilled me right out of the club circuit. Haven't been able to work a club since."

The knock on the door caused Shirlee to spin around and open it. She snatched the bottle from Terrible's hands and slammed the door in his face before the old man could utter a word. She tore open the bottle sealer with her teeth and tipped the bottle neck directly to her scarlet lips. She took such a long slug, Glen thought she'd never put it down. However, with a gasping cough she finally did lower it and refilled her glass. "That's better," she said.

Suddenly it wasn't better. She leaned her hands heavily on the sink area as another cough shook her body and she became violently sick in the sink.

Glen slipped out of the trailer while Shirlee was so engaged.

On the outside Glen took in deep gulps of fresh air and then realized what the strange smell was that he had been breathing for the last hour.

Stale whiskey filled air in the home of a very lonely person.

CHAPTER EIGHTEEN

Glen walked back through the Side Show tent to enter again upon the mid-way. A strange silence had come over the entire carnival area. At first Glen couldn't fathom what he heard or was not hearing as the case was. Then it slowly dawned on him. The work was done. The giant hammers, the saws, and the yelling of the work men were at least silenced. The carnival was set up—ready for business later that night.

It was the time for rest.

"If only the rain holds off," said Glen almost aloud as he looked to the gray threatening sky.

Glen made his way back to his trailer. The drinks with Shirlee had made him a bit woozy—enough so he figured another would do him no harm and probably would be of some help. He supposed Bill Greater must have left some whiskey around and his supposing turned out to be correct. There was a half filled bottle of good bourbon in the safe along with the record books and insurance papers.

Glen put the bottle and a glass on his desk. He poured a quick one and after sipping off it he studied the remainder of the amber liquid in the glass. "Poor lush," he reflected, then sat the glass down and swung around to his suit case which he opened immediately. Slowly he took out the high heeled shoes, the brassiere, the set of slacks and Glenda's beautiful white angora turtle neck sweater. He let the fur of the soft angora sweater rub smoothly across his cheeks. He buried his face into it until a hurried feeling encased his groin; deep down inside.

Glen stripped off his own clothes as fast as he could, tossing each garment carelessly away from him. Just as quickly he slipped into the female attire. Moments later, with her long-haired wig adjusted to perfection, Glenda added a last dab of lipstick to her lips.

"Now we can really talk on the same level."

Glenda spun around to see Shirlee standing in the open doorway. She entered and closed the door behind her, permitting her hand to snap the lock into place. "That's one of the most beautiful sweaters I've ever seen," she said during her cross to Glenda. She put her long, slender arms up around his neck and drew Glenda's head and lips down to hers.

"Glenda," she moaned. "It is Glenda, isn't it?"

CHAPTER NINETEEN

The great mid-way was as bright and colorful as the gaudy posters in town had boasted it would be. The fantastic ad-banners flew high over tents and concessions, with concessionaires and barkers hacking their wares and attractions. The rides clamored on squeaky gears. Hundreds of people, the suckers, roamed the fair way; paid their money; rode the rides; viewed the attractions; were horrified by the gigantic snakes; oh'd and ah'd at the Egyptian dancing girls; were amazed at the fire eater; angered at a supposedly cheating game man; screamed with excitement while in the airplane swing; even more screaming from the loop-the-loop. The great white way was in full swing.

In the trailer Glenda had once more become Glen. He smiled broadly. The storm had held. If it would only hold off a few hours longer he felt he would be well on the way to recouping some of his investment. That would be a welcome change for a change—everything had been going out and nothing coming in. That crap had to cease.

A glaring flash of lightning with a follow up crash of a thunder clap shattered the gaiety of the outside activity. Glen spun around, wide eyed, from his desk to face the closed door. He sprung to his feet, threw open the door. Ernie and Mac stood there, just about to knock. Glen looked to them, then worriedly to the deep blackness of the

107

sky. Another streak of lightning cut the darkness. Mac and Ernie both looked skyward, then back to Glen.

"Guess we'll collect our *rent* now, Mr. Starr."

"It's only eight o'clock."

Ernie looked skyward again before he spoke. "Looks like midnight ain't gonna get here tonight." He looked down at Glen again. "Now we don't want to be hard about this." He had feigned tenderness.

"Just one way," injected Glen knowingly.

"If that's the way you'd like to say it."

"Two hundred. Get it up, buster," chimed in Mac. "We got other things to do before the rain hits."

Another worry clouded Glen's face. "You really think it'll rain?"

Lightning flashed and the thunder roared.

Ernie indicated the sky. "Does that answer your question?"

"Could be heat lightning."

"Not this time of the year." Ernie smiled wickedly. "Gonna be worse than last night too, I'd bet."

Mac put his hands defiantly on his hips. "Are we about to stay here all night jawin' with this punk, Ernie?" He snapped on Glen again. "Look buster, dig up the two C's—then we'll be on our way."

"Until tomorrow," added Ernie.

"Yeah—that's right, Ernie. Until tomorrow. Just thought of somethin' . . . Maybe the sky, *tomorrow*, will let us wait until midnight to collect our—*rent*."

Then with an even greater flash of lightning and roar of thunder, the sky opened up. The rain hit in a fantastic down pour.

"Damn it punk," screamed Mac. "Get up that cash—now!"

Glen dug into his pocket. He came up with a roll of paper money. Mac grabbed the cash out of his hand counted off several bills and slapped the rest back into Glen's hand. He glanced with a deep glare to Glen's eyes as he spit out his words.

"I just took an extra fifty, just because you kept us here jawin' until we got wet."

Mac and Ernie turned and raced back to their patrol car; a moment more and the patrol car sped off leaving Glen standing just inside his opened trailer doorway. The fire of anger in his eyes deepened to searing proportions. He wouldn't take much more of their crap. Glenda had killed before. She could be called on to do it again. Glenda had always killed for money—but then wasn't this for money—besides these were two hateful men.

The thoughts of revenge raced through his mind rapidly, a matter of seconds. The spell suddenly broke as the noisy, screaming crowd raced out of the fair grounds, running for their cars out in the parking area. There wasn't a thought in any of the hundreds of their minds to take temporary cover because each knew this would be no temporary storm. This was going to last. The force of the near windless rain already was turning the mid-way into thick mud-muck.

Glen watched the action of those people with a sinking heart. His first day. Already a total loss.

One by one the rides ceased to move. The music and blaring loud speakers became silent. Then the lights were gone. The voices of the barkers and the concessionaires were stilled. A few minutes more, after the last automobile had gone, only the sounds of a poker game off in one of the tents broke the stillness of the rain swept night.

Glen pulled up a chair and sat in the doorway. With his head in his hands he looked out over the scene. A scene of storm drenched emptiness.

CHAPTER TWENTY

If the rain could get any worse it did by the time Glen parked his car in front of Pug-Ugly Happy Chandler's bar in town. He got out of the car and ran the few steps to the doorway and entered.

The bar was vacant except for Happy Chandler, who was behind the bar and the old taxi driver asleep at his favorite table in the back out of everyone's way. Happy Chandler looked up immediately at Glen's entrance, his face breaking out into a wide grin. "Well hello there new owner."

Glen crossed to stand at the bar. "Hi Happy." There was no happiness in his tone.

Happy let the smile leave his face. "Too bad about the rain washin' you out like this." He paused over Glen's unadorned drink as he talked. "Specially on your first night as the new owner."

"How'd you hear I took over?"

"Not much I don't hear. Pretty small town."

"Mac and Ernie?"

He nodded his head. "They stopped in awhile back."

"The bastards." A slight twinge of Glenda's tone. When he was angry he found Glenda slipping through more and more and for some reason he cared less and less. Glenda had such a beautiful voice.

"You gettin' a cold?"

"Could be."

Happy Chandler shoved the glass of straight

111

whiskey across to him. "Better slug this one down. You oughta take it with hot water, but I ain't got none. Maybe it'll work just as good this way. Can't run a carnival if you ain't got a voice to do it with."

Glen did slug down the whiskey. "Gimme a bottle over at the table." As an after thought, he said, "Bring two glasses."

"Sure."

Glen moved to a table in a dark portion of the bar. Happy Chandler, with the bottle and two glasses, joined him there a moment later.

Glen looked up to him as he put the glasses down on the table. "No business for either of us tonight. Might just as well join me, Happy."

"Now that's mighty nice of you. What do they call you anyway?"

"Glen."

"Yeah. You never did say last night."

"Glen Starr. . . From down Florida way."

"Florida—and no accent."

"Everyone in Florida doesn't have an accent."

"Guess you're right at that." He poured the double shot glasses to the brim. "Good luck to you."

"I need it." Glen was serious.

They drank up. This time Glen poured.

A girl in her late twenties, wearing a red rain coat and red beret, moved in from the street. Without removing her coat or shaking the rain from it she walked directly to the bar. Happy Chandler stood up.

112

"Be right back."

"Who is she?" Glen was fascinated.

"Neighborhood girl. Streets. Guess her business is as bad as ours tonight." He laughed his booming laugh and walked away to the bar.

Glen found he didn't want to take his eyes from the girl. She actually was beautiful but even at that her face showed a few of the lines which come from worldly experience; of a tiredness that her profession could never help to erase. Maybe it was the red rain coat that attracted him. Or the long blonde hair which spilled so freely from under her beret. It must be that.

It had been a long time since he'd lain with a real woman. He could almost feel her soft body next to his. Never naked of course. How he detested the naked body, his or anyone else's. But put some sexy things together—soft—frilly material. Then, there was that deep feeling in his groin—and now, there it was again, one which only Glenda's wardrobe, or her type of wardrobe could ease.

Maybe this girl could be brought around to his way. It was so far back to his office and Glenda's clothes. This one was so close—and she was a street walker. He could pay.

Once, back in New York, he had the same feeling in his groin and he had picked up a street girl; her clothes foremost in his mind, and he took her to her apartment. When he asked to wear her nighties and a negligee she had laughed so hard he ran out of the room. It took him a full two years before he ever ventured such an experience again.

The more he stared at the girl in red, the more he visualized the things she wore underneath. Her room. Her bed. Oh God, her wardrobe.

Happy Chandler came back and sat down in the chair he had vacated a few minutes before. He took up his glass as Glen spoke. "You know her?" His mouth had become dry.

"Sure. A street dame like I said. Name's Rose Graves. Funny name, huh? Most folks around call her Red because she almost always wears red."

"Think she'd take me on tonight?"

"Hey—this ain't no whore house." He kept his voice low.

"For a friend?"

"For a friend I should kick her outta here. How do you know what she's got between her legs that you might not like to take back to the carnival with you?" Happy Chandler saw Glen was serious. He broke into a grin. "Sure. For a friend. I was only kiddin'. She's a clean one. I'd bet on it."

He got up and walked to the girl where they had a whispered conversation. She gave a shrug, got off the stool and both moved back to Glen. Glen got up politely.

"Meet Mr. Starr, Miss Grace. He'd like you to drink with him."

"Sure," she said simply and sat down. "A name's a name. Yours is Glen."

As Glen reseated himself Happy Chandler moved away, back to his bar.

"Whiskey?"

"I dislike beer, except if I have to pay for my own drinks, then usually I let it sit on the bar." Her voice was as smooth and as pleasant as her face was lovely.

Glen used the glass left by Happy Chandler for her drink. He filled hers first, then replenished his own.

"I'm paying . . . drink up."

She did so. Glen immediately refilled it. "Why don't you take your coat off"

"I'd only have to put it on again when *we* leave."

"We?"

"That's what you have in mind, ain't it?"

"I—I guess so."

"Don't you know?"

"It's what I have in mind."

"I'm a business girl. Good hard business. I'm sociable for a price—just understand that." She paused to light a cigarette. "Your place—or mine?"

"I'm on my way out to the fair grounds. But I have a car."

"My place then. It's just around the corner."

"So business-like." He said the words silently to himself. It was the same as he had remembered such women. But he knew she must have something interesting in her clothes closet—and certainly some dainties of a desirable nature. just to look at her was enough to realize she still had some self respect for her clothing. She'd just have to

115

have something to please him. All his thoughts were centering more violently around such. His groin was beginning to ache. Something would have to be done soon. "I'll bring a bottle," he finally said aloud.

"Make it two. The rain might last all night."

"Okay."

"Shall we go?"

"Now?"

"Why drink in a slop place like this. We can be more comfortable at my place."

"I'm ready."

Glen got up then helped her to her feet. Glen turned leaving the half empty bottle on the table, but as he moved to Happy Chandler at the bar Rose scooped up the bottle and fit it under her arm, then she joined Glen at the bar.

"Two bottles," ordered Glen.

"You leavin' already?"

"Wet night—the best place for anybody is a nice room, good company, a bottle or two of whiskey and perhaps a warm bed." Glen forced a smile to curl the corners of his lips. "I think I have all four right here."

Happy Chandler burst out in his fantastic deep bellied laugh again. "I bet you have at that." Then he shrugged. "With you two going I might just as well close up. Ain't nobody else gonna show up on a night like this."

But Happy Chandler was wrong. No more than the words were out of his mouth and the paper bag covered bottles were put into Glen's hands, the old drunk, Henry, pushed his way through the door, slouched over the bar and slurringly demanded a drink.

Happy Chandler shrugged again. "Now I suppose I'm stuck until Mac and Ernie get here!"

Glen snapped his eyes questioningly to Happy Chandler. Happy Chandler indicated Old Henry with his thumb. "Sure. Remember, I told you last night. Sooner or later they always show when old Henry's out on the town and shows up here."

Glen turned quickly to Rose. "Let's get out of here."

"You don't like cops?" She was calm but pointed in her question.

"I don't like Mac and Ernie. Let's get out of here."

"I like you more and more all the time, lover. Those two are on my shit list too. Cops! Those two ain't any bettern' my pimp they locked up the last month." She had sneered her words through clenched teeth. "Let's go, honey."

"See you later," waved Pug-Ugly Happy Chandler as he moved off toward old Henry.

CHAPTER TWENTY-ONE

Mac and Ernie pulled their patrol car in to the curb just as Glen and Rose came out of the bar.

"Well if that ain't a likely pair," said Ernie, loud enough to be heard.

"Yeah. Birds of a feather. Hey Rose. Maybe he can do better for you than Herbie did. Herbie's gonna be away a long time. You'll be needin' a new—manager." Mac's words were brutal; his follow up cynical laugh was even more so.

"Don't be hard on them Mac. After all. Everybody's got to make a living. Everybody to what they're educated for." Ernie joined in the laughter.

"Something to do with parents, I hear," added Mac.

Glen started to take a step forward but was quickly restrained by a light hand from Rose. "Don't let them get under your skin Glen. That's what they want. You'd be found in an alley or thrown in jail on some trumped up charge."

Glen knew immediately she was right. Dalten Van Carter's dying face shot across his mind's eye for the first time in days. He winced at the feeling of terror it gave him. The thoughts of jail bars horrified him. Then another terrifying punch struck his senses. The syndicate would certainly find him. If so, he would face more than some quick death.

"You better listen to her bright boy!" There was no more humor in Ernie's voice this time.

Both cops opened their own doors at the same time. They moved quickly across the rain drenched street to the protection of Happy Chandler's wide doorway where Glen and Rose were standing.

"Why don't you get off my back?" steamed Rose.

"You're angling for another trip to the farm, broad."

"You'd like that wouldn't you, Mac?"

"The head matron out there would. Heard you and she had quite a go at it last time."

She raised her hand to slap the cop's face, but this time it was Glen who restrained her. "Now whose skin are they getting under?"

"Bright boy is sure brightenin' up, ain't he Ernie." He turned back to Glen and Rose. "You landed that slap, bitch and you'd be facing a gang bang down at the drunk tank." Mac slammed his way through Happy Chandler's door and let it slam shut.

Ernie looked with hard eyes to Glen. "After you get through with her, buster—there's a *pro* station over next to the Sheriff's office." He opened the door. "See you out at the fair grounds tomorrow." He went in, letting the door close easily behind him.

"Dirty, no good, mother grabbin' bastard," Rose hissed almost silently. Then aloud she said, "This place suddenly got a shit stink about it. Where's your car?"

Glen pointed to his car just in front of the

police car.

"There."

Without another word she stormed out into the rain. She got into the car and slammed the door. Glen made a dash for his side.

CHAPTER TWENTY-TWO

Rose Graves had what must be called an apartment, certainly an inexpensive one, but nevertheless a three room apartment; living room, bedroom and small kitchen, which at the moment of their entrance was closed off by a set of drawn curtains. Rose immediately put one of the bottles on a coffee table in front of a divan, then took the remaining two, one full, one half, into the kitchen. She returned a moment later with two glasses which she put next to the bottle. It was only then she took off her red rain coat and beret which she tossed over a wooden chair near the kitchen.

Glen nearly drooled at the red satin, knee length cocktail dress she had been wearing beneath the rain coat. Even her drop earrings, necklace and bracelet were of a red glass. She leaned over to open the bottle and pour the whiskey into both glasses.

"Bet you even wear red undies." Glen had a warm smile on his face.

She looked slyly up to him from her drink pouring action; she was getting to like this guy. More than just for a night's interlude and the money it would afford her.

"Didn't Happy tell you I was called Red." She lifted the drinks and handed Glen one. "Now drink your *red* eye." She smiled even more broadly as she slipped down onto the divan. "Drink your drink, honey—There's more where that came from." A deeper grin. "You should know—You paid for it." She kicked off her shoes, shooting them high into the air; one at a time. Each landed harmlessly on the rug near the door. "Say," she said as Glen picked up his glass of whiskey. "Let's take off." Almost as suddenly she stood up, unzipped her dress and let it fall to a circle at her feet. She stood revealed in red satin brassiere and red satin flare leg panties.

"Like 'em?"

"I love them." Again more meaning than he let on. "I bet you've even got a red crotch."

Without another word she dropped her panties. "Just call me *Red*—like everybody else." She kicked the panties into the air. They fell onto Glen's lap. Unconsciously he began to caress them lightly.

Rose walked into her bedroom, unsnapping her brassiere as she moved. She was gone only a minute and when she returned she wore a red satin, wrap around robe. Almost immediately she sank back down on the divan letting both sides of the satin robe fall away from her legs. All she had below the waist line came into sight and she did nothing about covering it up again.

"Happy tells me you bought the carnival. You must be very rich," she said more as a matter of conversation than for information.

"Took just about everything I had to buy it." Then quickly. "Oh, I'm not totally broke. I can last alright for a while. Then too. The rain can't last forever." He paused. "The carnival will pay

122

off in time."

She refilled their glasses. "Sure it will. Come sit beside me." She patted the section of the divan directly next to her.

Glen got up from his chair. He walked quickly to the position she had indicated for him. She took his hand and put it on the inside of her naked thigh. It was hot. Her body heat promised of more goodies to come. She moved his hand slowly up and down, back and forth. She leaned against the back of the divan. Her eyes closed in the ecstasy of the moment. A light whimpering came from between her closed lips. A sound which belied the enjoyment her body now possessed. Her hand moved his more rapidly. Then it was over as quick as it had started. She let go of his hand; reached up and dragged his head down to hers. Her tongue darted in and out of his mouth. Her hot breath came out in deep gasps—"Not yet, lover—not yet . . ." she whispered, locking her lips to his.

When she permitted their lips to part she said, softly, "Take your clothes off, honey."

Glen stood up. "Let me—Let me have one of your robes. I don't like parading around in the nude."

"Okay," she said simply; killed off her drink and went into her bedroom. She returned, carrying a blue satin robe just as Glen was about to remove his nylon, pink chemise. He had always worn a chemise and panties under his otherwise masculine outer clothing. She stopped dead in her tracks in the doorway for a long moment, her eyes fastened on the female undies. She tossed him the blue satin robe as she spoke. "I should have known. The plucked eye brows. Those long nails with the pearl polish. I sure should have known." She crossed to him as he slipped into and belted the robe around his middle. She refilled her drink as she spoke again. "Pretty undies dearie." She drank. "What do we do now? Make lesbian love?" She sunk down onto the divan, a bit of a pout on her lips.

"Want me to leave?"

"Why? You're paying for my time."

"Can't we put it on more friendly terms?" He sat down beside her again.

"Could be—when I get more drunk. Maybe you'd like one of my nighties to go with that robe—or maybe my fox trimmed negligee?"

"Damn it to hell yes," he wanted to scream, but instead he said softly, "Maybe later."

She laughed. He didn't like that. "Don't laugh." He slammed to his feet, went to his jacket and took a hundred dollar bill from his wallet. He walked back to her and tossed the bill on the table in front of her. She nearly choked on her whiskey. "Suppose that will stop your laughing?" His voice was hard.

She leaned forward. Her face a mask of amazement. She picked up the bill for an even closer examination. "This—This is ten times my price."

"Maybe I'll be ten times the bother."

"Honey. For a hundred bucks you can be all

the bother you want. For a hundred bucks you can wear anything in my wardrobe—Treated anyway you want." She refilled her glass again. "We'll do it anyway, anywhere you want? And I'll do anything you want. Maybe some you haven't even heard of. We can go in the bedroom, the kitchen sink if you want. Believe me I know how to please you. I may be small time. But I've had all the experience you can think of."

He sat down beside her again.

"I'd like the nightie you spoke of."

"Sure—Sure—and a pair of slippers. I have a pair with heels that will fit you—would you like that?"

"Yes." He was quick to add, "Will you wear a nightie also—with your robe?"

"If that's what you want. I'll only be a minute." She went back into the bedroom.

Glen slipped out of the robe and stripped down to his nylon panties. He considered them a long moment then slipped them off and put on the red satin ones she had just discarded, then finished his first complete drink. He was refilling his glass as she returned carrying the two night gowns; one blue and one red, each matching the robes. He stood there in the red panties, drank his whiskey and watched her take off the robe, slip into the clinging satin night gown, then replace the robe over it. This done and the robe belted again, she went to him. Their lips met. Slowly her hands went down his naked sides. They slipped into the top of his panties. She was slowly lowering them.

Glen slipped the blue nylon nightie down over his head as her searching lips found his boyish nipples; her hot tongue seared his navel. He reached over, picked her up and carried her into the bedroom. She was already moaning with desire. "Sweet love, sweet love," she moaned. "Oh my boy, my girl, my sweet love. Take me. Take me as you want me . . ."

CHAPTER TWENTY-THREE

The gray morning light streamed through the bedroom window. During the night the rain had let up, but now it was hitting with force again and this time it was accompanied by a heavy wind. The droplets hit the window pane with a driving force causing little cracking noises. The sudden noise of it woke Glen with a start. It took a full minute for his sleep groggy brain to realize where he was, then he sat bolt upright in bed and looked around. The other side, where Rose had been, was empty. A slight chill shook his bare arms and shoulders where the nightie did not cover. A wonderful smell of cooking bacon and eggs gained entrance into his nostrils at that point. "Rose," he called lightly.

"Just a minute, honey," she answered from off in the kitchen area. And it was only a minute. She came into the bedroom wearing red slacks, red shoes, a red pull over sweater and a red ribbon in her beautifully fluffed out hair. "I'm cooking us some breakfast." She crossed to the closet where she took out a red marabou bed jacket which she tossed to him. "You'd better put this on Glenda— It's quite chilly this morning."

Glen did so gladly and immediately felt a thanks for its warmth. The weather had turned very cold—must have been due to all the rain.

"Only heat I've got in this joint is the kitchen stove and that just barely heats the kitchen." She had gone to the dresser where she removed a set of satin, gray lounging pajamas and tossed them to a chair near the bed. "Better put these on when you get up, with the bed jacket you'll be warm enough."

"I'd better get back to the fair grounds."

"Nonsense. What can you do in all this rain?"

Glen looked to the window where the rain hit loudly.

"It's even worse than last night," she moved toward the door. "You'll find some dainties and a set of falsies in the bottom drawer if you want them." Then she was gone.

Glen hooked the top most hook on the fluffy bed jacket, then leaned back against the head board. The beating of the rain against the window seemed to be lulling him with its rhythmic sounds.

What a night it had been. His body should feel tortured from all the action it took but instead he felt relaxed; spent but pleasingly relaxed. The marabou bed jacket felt good to his touch as his fingers caressed the feathers. Whow! What a night. Rose had turned out to be as good in bed as his former lay, Mona, who "understood." Even more so since Rose knew all the angles; the tricks of the trade. He smiled broadly as he set his mind in remembrance. He looked to the night stand where he could see an empty whiskey bottle and the second with about an inch of the amber liquid still remaining. He reached over, uncorked it and drank the remainder. After smacking his lips in appreciation of good liquor he put the bottle back on the night stand. Funny. They had drank two Fifths of booze between them and there were no ill after effects. He burped. An embarrassed Glenda like giggle escaped his lips. "Now that's not very ladylike," he said softly.

"Did you say something honey?" She called from the kitchen.

"No—Nothing important."

"Breakfast will only be another couple of minutes."

"Take your time. No hurry."

Glen took a cigarette from the stand and lit it with a lighter also found there. He took great care in lighting it because a spark could well set the feathered bed jacket on fire.

"White toast all right?" she called again.

"Perfectly."

"Good. It's all I have," she giggled as if she had made a great joke.

Glen got out of bed putting on the high heeled fur trimmed slippers as he did so. He picked up the satin lounging pajamas, selected a set of undies and the falsies from the dresser then continued on into the small bath where he took a quick shower. When he had finished and dried off he quickly put on the lounging outfit and marabou jacket and then joined Rose in the kitchen at the breakfast table.

"You smell nice," she ventured.

"I found your perfume." He sat down. "The food in here smells good too."

Rose put both plates of bacon, eggs and fried

potatoes on the table in silence. She spoke again as she poured coffee into their cups. "The two hundred dollar special, lover," she said in jest then sat down opposite Glen.

"We'll have more together. I like you Rose."

She reached across to hold his hand in hers affectionately. "I like you too Glenda. Last night. In the beginning I didn't think I would. Give you a little and get you out of here. Like maybe it was a *change of pace thing* for your kind."

"The hundred bucks changed that, huh?" His voice was light, almost of self pity.

"Can't lie to you about that. I was pretty hot when I saw you standing there in your pink chemise. Brought back too many unpleasant memories. The hundred bucks wouldn't let me act any other way but to take you on. I put up a hell of a show there for awhile. I never got a hundred bucks a night in my life, never thought I would. Even then, when you carried me to bed and you were against my body it was like layin' with my sister. You heard what Mac said to me last night about the prison farm and the Matron out there. If you wanted decent treatment there you took care of the Matron. If you ain't a lesbian when you go in you sure know what the score is all about by the time you come out." The hatred which had been building in her slowly began to subside. "Especially if you're young and pretty and have a good shape or have the cash money to buy out of such things. Money's the only thing you can use to buy out of a party with her and her bastard guards."

"It must have been lousy for you," said Glen when she stopped long enough to take a sip of coffee.

"Lousy! That's little enough word for it. Work the fields or the mill all day then entertain the troops for most of the night. Maybe now you can understand a little of what I felt last night when I first saw you, like that in drag. Sure. For the hundred I guess I could stand anything. Then a strange thing happened. Your tenderness to me. Clinging to your soft yet commanding body. Something came over me that changed my every feeling toward you. I knew then I wanted you with all my senses. Hour after hour, last night, I longed for just one more time. Just one more time. I didn't want the night to ever end. I never wanted you to leave. I've had people of your strange desires before, I cannot deny it, even worse, but not with the talent for pure love you possess." She finished the remainder of her coffee. "Glenda," she said suddenly. "Take me with you when you leave."

Glen, transfixed by her words could only stare.

Rose hastened to add, "Please, Glenda. Take me with you. Oh not as a legal wife, I know you don't want that sort of an arrangement. I could cook for you. We could make your special kind of love. I could work in one of the shows." She got up to pace the floor. "There is nothing here for me in this town. I'd be a small time hooker the rest of my life, until I die. The cops know me too well. The only reason I can stay off the farm is because I give it to Ernie and Mac every weekend. With hate and vengeance I give it to them. I tried playing it cold—stiff as a board with them once. They beat me into submission."

"Those dirty swine," cut in Glen.

She came around behind him and put her arms around his neck. She buried her chin deep into the marabou feathers at the nape of his neck. "I've got to get away from here before I go completely mad or worse. I've thought often of ending it all."

Glen pulled her tightly around to face him. She dropped to her knees and curled her arm and head on his knees.

"Don't talk like that, Rose."

"It's the way I really feel."

"A carnival season only lasts a few months in the summer."

"By that time I can have enough money to land in a big town where maybe I can have a chance."

"For the same kind of business?"

She stood up quickly. "What else do I know?"

"It's a tough life."

"Any tougher than here for two—three—five—ten bucks a night."

Glen sipped his coffee in deep thought as she continued. "Any place is better than that. Maybe I could get to Hollywood."

"There's hundreds—thousands of girls with that same idea going there every year."

"I've got to give it a try. I've got to try something. You see what it's like for me here."

"Well you do have a point there."

"Now your eggs are cold."

"That's alright. I wasn't really hungry anyway."

"More coffee?"

"Yes, please."

She poured the coffee into both their cups again. "Will you take me?"

"With the rain the way it is I don't know how long the show will last. If I have to sell out we'd both be in worse shape than we are now."

"Nothing is worse than my present condition."

Glen went into deeper thought again then suddenly stood up and crossed to his jacket. He took another hundred dollars from it then recrossed to sit down again. "Get me a piece of paper, a pencil and an envelope, will you please Rose?"

"Sure." Rose was puzzled but did as she was asked. She laid the articles in front of Glen.

Glen wrote down a phone number quickly folded the bill inside the paper and sealed both into the envelope. He handed it to Rose as he spoke. "I'll take you with me," he said. "On one condition."

The light in her eyes was only overshadowed by the happiness in her face. "Anything!"

"There's a hundred dollars and the phone number of a friend in New York. A girl. She's in the know and can get you started right—if at that time you still want this kind of life only for higher stakes. The hundred is bus fare. I don't want you to ever use it until it becomes necessary. This way, anything happens along the way you can always make it to New York." He paused to drink more coffee.

She started to speak but Glen stopped her again with his soft tones. "Don't thank me, Rose. You might think, now, I'm doing you a favor—but in time perhaps you'll hate me for what I am doing."

"Never—never!" She came around to throw her arms around his neck.

"We'll see." He kissed her, long, hard, wet.

Her body began to rub hotly, her wool against his satins. She squeezed his falsies as if she were working at the real thing. Her right hand suddenly dropped downward to his legs; pointedly. "Bed—bed—bed—bed," she whimpered, her mouth racing over his—

Then the knock on the door. Loud. Insistent.

They sprang apart, their fires of passion leaving them immediately. For a long moment they stared wide eyed at the door. The insistent knocking repeated itself. They snapped to look at each other. Their voices came in frantic whispers.

"Mac and Ernie?" Glen's features had frozen as he looked up and down surveying the female attire he was wearing.

"I don't know. I don't know." She was near panic.

"Rose . . . Rose . . . Let me in quick—" It was the voice of Happy Chandler just as insistent as his knocking had been. "It's important. Let me in. I gotta see you right away." He was racing his words. There seemed to be panic in his door muffled voice also.

"It's Happy." She breathed a bit easier.

"What can he want?"

"I ain't never made him. It must be important to come up here. He's never been up here before. I'd better see what he wants."

Glen grabbed up his trousers and shirt, then raced into the bedroom, taking off the marabou bed jacket on the run.

Rose moved to the door and opened it. A nervous Happy Chandler stood there. He pushed his way into the room closing the door quickly behind him. He dragged a big handkerchief from his pocket to wipe the rain from his face as he rushed his words. "Is that carnival fellow here Rose? I gotta find him quick."

"Why do you want him?""

"He seems like a nice sort. I figure it's my place to find him and tell him quick."

"Tell him about what, Happy?"

"He's got trouble out at the carnival."

Glen came out of the bedroom fast. "What's wrong, Happy?"

"Thought I'd find you here Mr. Starr when you wasn't out at the fair grounds. There's plenty of trouble out there."

"What kind of trouble?"

"Seems a couple of town folks went out there last night; got into a poker game with some of your boys."

"So? "

"Somebody yelled crooks. Fight started. Your

135

men against them others. After they wrecked the tent, the fight went outside. Real rough the way I hear it; knives and clubs. Anyway it gets over to the ride area after tearin' down a coupla concession booths. Three of them land in one of the Ferris Wheel cars. Somebody else hits the switch. Round and round she goes. Then it happens. That damned wheel plain falls right off its hooks. Killed all three of them. Mac and Ernie'll be flyin' into you—thought you needed a friend to tell you first."

Glen dashed around madly grabbing his jacket and rain coat. "Thanks, Happy."

"I'd better get. I don't want Mac and Ernie thinkin' I'm gone against them. I gotta live here."

"Sure—sure—You go ahead. Thanks again, Happy. I'll try to make it up to you."

"Good luck Mr. Starr." He went out quickly, closing the door behind him.

Rose put her arms around Glen. "They can't tie you into it Glen—You were with me here all night. They can't, can they?"

"I don't know, honey. . . I don't know. Look. I've got to get out there. If things go bad, remember that envelope I gave you." He turned to the door.

"Wait." Rose ran to the bedroom. She came back in seconds. Standing in front of Glen again she handed him her red beret. "A small part of me will always be with you." Helpful smile. "Keep the rain off your head."

"I'll come back later. If I can." He left quickly.

CHAPTER TWENTY-FOUR

Glen arrived at the fair grounds just as the morgue wagon was driven through the main gate. Glen parked at his trailer and trudged his way on foot through the deep mud and pouring rain, the remainder of the way to the ride area, where he found the scene to be in even worse destruction than he had been informed.

The giant wheel in falling had crashed into the airplane ride which in turn had fallen on top of the girlie show tent where all electrical wire had been severed causing the tent to burn, costumes, stage and all equipment. Only a miracle of the rain had kept the fire from spreading further.

Both the wheel and the airplane rides were a mass of twisted, unrepairable steel.

Volunteer firemen were still spraying smoldering parts of the girlie show attraction. Big hatted deputies in rain slickers kept back crowds of townspeople and carnival folks. Electrical help were tying off wires in several sections; extremely dangerous work considering all the water they were forced to work in. As Glen watched, one of those electricians must have gotten a little shock of one kind or another because he was heard to curse violently above all the other noise.

Mac and Ernie were seen with an elderly man in a big hat and rain slicker, amid the twisted wreckage. Glen got a cold chill of sudden fright which made his whole frame shudder. He wanted to turn and run. But run where? This time he couldn't hope to get away. He was known by too many. Almost everything there was to know about him. His height. His weight. His hair color, eyes, even the make and color and license of the car he drove. It would be little trouble, also, to find Bill Greater and even see the style of handwriting he had by examining the signature he had put on the purchase contract. He wouldn't get five miles in any direction this time if he turned and ran. He wished he had a drink right then.

Glen summoned up all his courage. He made his way laboriously through the twisted, torn wreckage until he stood beside the three lawmen. The third, Glen was to learn, was town sheriff Abner Sales.

Only the old sheriff looked up to him as he approached. It was, however, apparent both Mac and Ernie were aware of his presence but neither would give him the satisfaction of recognition at that time. Both were accustomed to doing things as they saw fit and in their own good time. Glen was determined also to wait it out. He didn't have long to wait.

A man in a yellow rain slicker who had been inspecting the giant wheel gears and base construction, stepped into the group. "Can I talk to you a minute Ernie?" he asked.

"Sure Dan—You find something?"

"Could be. Come have a look anyway."

Ernie joined the man and they walked back to the gears out of ear shot. Glen turned to watch them. Almost immediately the two men had reached the base construction and gears, both went to their hunches in close investigation of those works. Glen unconsciously bit his thumb nail in perplexity. Mac's sudden voice in low, spaced words brought him around again.

"Mr. Starr. This here's sheriff Abner Sales." Mac looked to the old sheriff. "Mr. Starr owns this rag-bag, Sheriff."

The sheriff put his hand out to Glen for a friendly greeting but quickly drew it back as Mac spoke again.

"Save your formalities, Sheriff. You may be handcuffing this joker one of these days." Mac looked Glen up and down. "While you were playin' mamma and papa with Rose—looks like there was a playin' around goin' on out here. You may be in big trouble boy. Big trouble. Four men died here last night."

"Four?"

"Three in the wheel. One of our townspeople was also stabbed. He died before an ambulance got here." Mac reached under his slicker to bring out cigarettes and matches. He lit one before he continued. "Yes, sir. You could have real big trouble." He laughed. "You should have let old Bill Greater keep his damned flea bag."

Mac was still laughing when Ernie returned. Ernie glared for a long, silent, hate-filled minute at Glen. Glen felt his skin crawl, as if he were looking into the eyes of a deadly cobra, coiled and ready to strike. Out of the corner of his own eyes he could see the puzzled expression on the old sheriff's face and the sneering smirk on Mac's.

"Your equipment was rotten," Ernie finally said.

"Told you you might have big trouble, buster," chimed in Mac.

"The gears were gone. The base construction also snapped with the soft mud from this rain. The slightest slip in that base caused the gears to snap. The wheel then, out of control, rolled off its axle." Ernie shrugged. "Then those three men just rode it down and over. That's all she wrote."

"I'd call that criminal negligence—wouldn't you Sheriff?" inquired Mac.

"Just as you say Mac." Mac took a deep drag from his cigarette as he eyed the speaking sheriff.

"Yes sir. Big trouble. Guess you'll be going down town with us fella." Mac patted the portion of his rain slicker where his pistol was housed.

"Where do you get this criminal negligence bit?" Glen finally found his voice.

"Well what does it look like to you?" Ernie pointed off to the man in the yellow rain slicker who was still bending over the gears. "See that fella' over there? Well he's a city engineer and he says that wheel should have been condemned years ago and that with a further look-see he's gonna find other rides in the same unseemly condition." Ernie was shouting. "You say that ain't negligence? Well he oughta know buster. He oughta know. That's what he's paid for—to know all about such things."

Glen's voice came on just as strong, just as

140

loud. "You just said it yourself. He should know. That stuff should have been condemned years ago. I only bought the carnival yesterday."

"You should have inspected the equipment before you bought it, ain't that right Sheriff?"

"Sounds to me like you're right, Ernie."

"You bet I am."

"I bought this carnival in good faith."

"What about insurance?" asked Mac, keeping his voice to an even level.

Certainly! The insurance! Why didn't he think of that before? There certainly wouldn't have been any insurance given if the equipment had been faulty. The rides couldn't have been set up in the first place if there hadn't been insurance. He had seen the insurance papers when he signed those sale papers. They rested now in his safe in the trailer. Some of the tension left his body.

"I have insurance. . ."

A quizzical look passed between Mac and Ernie.

"You have insurance?" said Ernie, still in the form of a question.

"Yes. In the safe. In my trailer. I'll get the papers. That'll prove your claim of criminal negligence is crazy. I'll get them."

"You don't have to prove anything to us fella. It's the judge you'll have to convince." Mac was still calm of tone.

"Am I under arrest?"

"We'll talk about that later. Maybe something can be arranged. Bail or something." Ernie's temper came back to normal. There was an underlying plan to his words.

"Well now Ernie—I don't know about that," intervened the old sheriff quite realistically. "We should take him in. You know the law."

"Now don't you fret none Abner. Besides. This is county. It's out of your territory. You don't have to worry none."

The old sheriff scratched his wet forehead thoughtfully. "Reckon you're right at that. This is your territory. Reckon as how it does come under your responsibility."

Mac moved in to put his arm confidently around the old man's shoulder. "Sure it is and we're gonna see that everything's carried out according to the letter of the law, ain't we Ernie?" He did not wait for an answer. "But then. If this joker ain't responsible so much as we first thought—then ain't no use in lockin' him up and causin' so much trouble for everybody. Now we want to be sure don't we—real sure?"

"Suppose you're right at that. Well. Ain't much for me to do out here. I'd best get back to town. The relatives of them killed fellas are gonna want a lot of talk from me."

"See you later Abner."

"Sure Mac. So long Ernie." The old man walked away.

The state patrolmen waited until the sheriff had driven off in his black coupe before continuing. It was Ernie who voiced first.

"Now remember—Mr. Starr—I ain't sayin'

you got them papers and I ain't sayin' you don't, 'cause you're in trouble no matter how you look at it. And them folks in town ain't gonna make it healthy for you—killin' off their relatives like you did. Now I think a fair exchange for three hours head start would be—let's say five thousand dollars."

"Five thousand dollars?" There was a bit of Glenda's squeal in his loud gasp.

Because of Glen's loudness neither Mac or Ernie caught Glenda's tone. "You keep your voice down!" demanded Ernie. "Maybe we should take you in anyway. Save ourselves a lot of grief."

Glen brought himself back to reality. He feared any kind of arrest. Fingerprints wouldn't lie. He was sure to be found out. "Now—Now wait fellas. I don't have five grand left. I can raise two. I spent it all on this outfit. You know what happened yesterday. I didn't make a cent. I was rained out. You guys took all the cash I took in at the box office."

"Raise it." Ernie came on strong.

"How long do I have?"

"Two hours—then you go in."

"Two hours." Glen's brain was working fast. If he had two hours he could be across the state line. There was a chance he could make it if he had another car.

"And don't get any ideas about taking off." Mac had seemed to read his mind. "You're gonna be watched all the time."

"Suppose you and me walk down to your trailer

now," suggested Ernie. "That where you keep your cash, ain't it. We'll just take that two grand on account."

"I have to go into town—sell my car."

"Sure," said Ernie. "And some junk dealer'll give you a grand or so for all this junk." His arm surveyed the carnival in its entirety. "See how easy it'll be. You can raise the five grand tonight."

"Soon's I pay you the cash you could run me in anyway. How do I know I can trust you?"

"You don't—but it's your only chance." A knowing glance passed between Mac and Ernie as Ernie had spoken. A glance that Glen caught and understood.

"You do that and I'll spill your whole rotten racket to anybody that'll listen."

Ernie hit him. Glen went down. He got up slowly, wiping the blood from his cut lip with the back of his hand. "I'll get the money," he said slowly.

CHAPTER TWENTY-FIVE

Ernie counted out every dollar of the two thousand Glen had taken from the safe. "Good to do business with you Mr. Starr. Just keep up the payments and we won't have to repossess the body." Ernie laughed at his own joke.

In the trailer doorway he turned back again. "We'll meet you outside of Happy Chandler's bar in two hours. Since you won't have a car it wouldn't make much sense having you walk all the way back out here." He pulled his slicker up around his neck and ventured out into the rain. The door swung shut behind him.

Shirlee, wearing a soggy fur coat of disputable origin, entered a moment later to find Glen with his head buried in his hands. She crossed to a bottle of whiskey on the table and poured stiff shots into two glasses also residing there. She went back to Glen and held one out. "Looks like you need this," she said.

Glen looked up. He took the glass and drained it.

"I guess you did at that." She took the empty glass, once more filled it, replaced it, full, into his hands. "Want to tell mamma all about it?"

"You can guess."

"What kind of a shake down is it?"

"Criminal negligence."

"Yeah . . . You know. They found one of those guys' arms fifty feet from the body." She drank and continued as if the whole thing was an everyday occurrence. "Tillie, our friend the Tattooed Lady really was cheating in that game. Caused the whole *Hey Rube*." Then Shirlee laughed. "Wait till those guys down at the morgue get a load of what she's hiding in her panties . . . Jane Doe becomes John Doe but fast. I'd sure like to see their faces. What a riot that's gonna be." She calmed. "Insurance might have helped you some."

"I've got insurance."

"Says who? Unless you were able to get it yesterday after you bought this rag-bag. Old Bill Greater hasn't been able to get insurance on those coffin filler rides in years. It's a wonder somebody hasn't been killed before."

"But I tell you he did have insurance. I have the papers over there in the safe." Glen was getting worried again.

"You'd better read the small print, dearie."

Glen shot out of his chair. While he searched through the papers in his safe for the insurance forms, Shirlee poured herself another drink. Then he found them. After reading them completely in his crouched position he got up and moved, a hopeless figure, back to the chair at his desk.

"That bad, huh?" inquired Shirlee.

"Worse."

"That's Bill Greater for you."

"According to these only the tent shows were insured."

"I repeat. That's Bill Greater for you."

"But . . . But how could the officials let him set

up without the protection of insurance—adequate insurance?"

"Bill Greater only played tank towns, rural areas where the so called officials are only looking out for a pay off. He'd flash those papers . . . See . . ." She pointed to the words. "There in big letters it says INSURANCE. Now what do you think those officials are gonna see better. The fine print held in his left hand or the green cabbage in his right?" She drank and refilled her glass again. "You're hooked honey." Her eyes narrowed. "If those cops gave you a deal, you'd better grab it. Could be your only chance." She killed off the drink and set the empty glass on the edge of his desk. "Well, lover. It was nice while it lasted. You were pretty good. Wish it could have gone on longer. But that's the way the cookie crumbles. I've got to get on the road—find a new show to team up with—there's still a lot of summer left, and a hard winter ahead." She closed the door behind her, then opened it once more. "Have heart, dearie . . . All is not lost. You can collect insurance on the girlie show tent." Then she was gone.

CHAPTER TWENTY-SIX

Rose opened the door almost immediately after Glen had knocked. Her kiss was insistent even before she had closed the door. "Oh, darling, darling. I was so worried."

Glen broke away long enough to close and lock the door, then she was in his arms again. "What did they do to you? I've been frantic all morning."

"I've got to leave town."

"I'll go with you."

"Not this time. I'll be traveling fast. I don't *want* to leave. I *have* to leave." Glen found he needed another drink. "Is there any whiskey left?"

"Yes, darling."

"Please get me some, will you?"

She was back in a minute with a water glass full. "Was it so bad?"

"Four people—killed. My carnival was wrecked. One tent burned. No insurance on the rides. They want me for criminal negligence. . . Just about as bad as it could get . . . I didn't know about the lack of insurance . . . That God damned crook Bill Greater didn't tell me."

"Bastards—Bastards . . . The whole world is made up of bastards. But I can still go with you."

"I honestly wish it were possible. This morning, under the cover of the carnival we could have chanced it. Now. Impossible. Rose. I'm going to level with you because I know I can trust you. I'm wanted for murder back east."

She gulped.

"I didn't do it. But I can't prove it. The only witness other than the murderer was also killed. Do you see why I can't be taken into custody?"

"Oh, my darling."

"And now do you see why I can't take you with me—not like this. I've got to travel alone and fast."

"I understand now, dearest . . . And I believe you incapable of murder."

"I wouldn't quite say that. But I'm innocent of what they want me for. Mac and Ernie were out there."

"The lousy bastards."

"It's a wonder they didn't take you in."

"They will unless I raise five grand in the next hour. I already gave them two thousand. I just sold the rides and tents to a junk dealer for another thousand. My car is worth about nine hundred on a quick deal. That still leaves eleven hundred I can't come up with."

"Honey, keep the thousand and your car. You don't think paying them blood money will let you off the hook, do you?"

"What other chance have I?"

"A lot more than turning up to pay them off. You pay and they take you off anyway."

"I told them if they pull any shit like that and I'd scream my head off about their blackmailing racket."

"Oh, you'd never see the inside of the county jail. That's fifty miles from here and there's a lot of desert on both sides. Perhaps one day some prospectors might stumble over your skeleton out there—that's the only way you'd ever be found. They wouldn't give you any chance to do your mouthing. Some honest cop might just take a notion to listen to you. No Glenda dear—You'd never see the inside of their jail."

"Checkmate."

"What's that?"

"The finish of a chess game."

"We ain't finished yet—not by a long shot."

"You've got something in mind?"

"Let me think a minute." In deep thought she went to the kitchen and poured a drink. When she returned she said, "Who besides me knows about Glenda?"

"The half-man, half-woman with the show."

"Is he loyal?"

"I don't really know. I think so."

"Where are your things? Especially your wig?"

"In the glove compartment of my car, down stairs."

"Then that part's out too . . . You've probably been followed. Maybe not. You told them you were going to sell your car?"

"Yes."

"Then why couldn't it be me you were selling the car to?" Her eyes narrowed as the plan formed.

"Go on."

"We'll go down stairs. I'll look the car over as if I'm going to buy it. I'll cover you while you get your wig, then make it look like I like the deal. We'll go back up here and get you changed.

150

Glenda will drive off right under their noses."

"Which leaves only one loop hole."

"What's that?"

"Mac and Ernie met Glenda on the road the night before last. So far there is no connection between her and me, but if they spot her in my car—they're not dumb—they'll put two and two together."

"Well that does present a stubborn problem. But let's get the wig first then figure out that part later."

Rose shrugged into her red rain coat and belted it. Glen took her beret from his pocket and handed it to her. "You'd better take your beret back for the time being. It's raining pretty hard out there." She smiled and adjusted the hat to her beautiful blonde hair.

In the street Glen showed his prospective buyer all around the car. He kicked the tires, honked the horn, then got in and started the motor. Rose got in beside him, an interested prospective buyer. They drove off slowly.

Half a block away Mac and Ernie's patrol car pulled out from the curb to follow at a safe distance.

Well under way Rose whispered to Glen. "Looks like Ernie and Mac didn't trust you to anybody else. They're right behind us. Give me the key to the glove compartment."

"The lock was sprung when I bought it—it's not locked."

Covering her movements she opened the glove

compartment and took out a tissue wrapped package. "This it?"

"Yes."

She slipped it up under her skirt and secured it in the tight waist band of her skirt. "We can go back now—I think this has been demonstration ride enough. But you'd better pull over to the curb first. Let me take the wheel—as if I'm getting the feel of it."

"Smart idea."

Glen pulled into the curb and got out his side of the car. He ran around the front to the passenger side trying to keep his eyes from drifting back the half block to where the patrol car had parked. He got in and Rose drove off immediately.

CHAPTER TWENTY-SEVEN

They had finished their second drink when Rose got the idea she had been searching her brain for. She stood up, her face changing from a deep frown to a broad, self pleased grin.

"You've got something."

She shook her head that she had. "And it's so simple I feel stupid for not having come up with it before." She quickly slipped her red sweater up over her head, tossed it to Glen then removed her slacks and shoes. "Put these on. You're going to be me. With these, my red rain coat and beret you'll appear to be me."

"What about my car? They know it."

"They just saw me buy it—so they think. What's wrong with me driving it off. "

"My wig is auburn? You're a blonde."

"You'll need it later to keep your disguise intact in the other places you'll land. In the meantime we'll push it till up into the beret. That's good too. It'll fill out the beret and appear as if you're keeping your hair dry. The rain may yet prove to be a blessing in disguise.

"By God, I think we'll make it." Glen was elated.

The smile faded from Rose's face. "Yeah, honey. You'll make it alright." She poured another shot of whiskey into her glass, a short one this time. "Ain't I the crazy one now? I want you with me so bad I can taste it and here I am showing you how to get away and maybe I'll never see you again."

Glen took her in his arms tenderly. A mist filled his eyes. Genuine tears were filling hers to overflow. "Don't feel that way Rose."

"I can't help it."

He held her close. "It won't be forever. I'll find you—wherever you are, I'll find you."

She pulled back slightly, letting a weak smile fitter through her tears. "I won't be hard to find." She indicated the envelope which was still on the table. "Just call the number you gave me. Your friend will know where I am."

"You're sure you want to go there?"

"Once I help you get away I can't stay here even if I wanted to, which I don't."

"Yeah, those two would lock you up and throw away the key. You'd never get off that prison this time."

"Where will you go?"

Glen pulled up his slacks and shoes. "That's something even I don't know." He spun away from her, removing his coat and jacket on the move. "Main thing now is to get started. Get out of this town." He removed his shirt.

"You'll need a brassiere."

"Yes. Everything, except my panties and chemise, which I have on, is in my suitcase."

She went into the bedroom with him.

Twenty minutes later Glenda adjusted her long auburn hair up under the red beret. Her face was made up to the expert degree which she had learned only through years of experiment and experience. She stood up from the vanity and walked to the bathroom door where she admired herself in the full length mirror. Appraisingly she smoothed the long lined, long sleeved, red sweater down over her skirt. She made sure the seams of her stockings were straight and cut neatly into the red patent leather shoes. With a last adjustment to a flashy cheap costume jewelry bracelet on her left wrist she turned to face Rose who stood wide eyed in amazement behind her. There was nothing of Glen left. The nails were painted a deep scarlet, matching the lipstick. Glenda's musical voice said, "Do you approve?"

"Whow!" She had never seen Glenda dressed and made up to such perfection before. "I've seen pictures of guys dressed up in girls' clothes before but you sure beat them all. I never seen any better nowhere—no place."

"There was a time my perfection in make-up meant the difference between success and failure. Maybe someday I'll tell you all about it." Glenda's voice came out full—rounded.

"You're absolutely beautiful. Get one of those operations like the boys have been doing in Europe and you'd be a real high priced hooker."

"I like things right where they are." Glen took her in his arms again.

She snuggled into the soft wool of Glenda's sweater. "I'll miss you so much."

"Perhaps we won't be separated for long. I'll come, or send for you as soon as I can." Glenda kissed her, smearing the lipstick on both their lips.

Rose took a handkerchief and cleaned Glenda's lips. "We should both wear the non-smear kind."

"I'll remember that in the future."

She hugged Glenda, close, again. "I don't suppose there would be time for one last bit—in the bedroom?"

Glenda looked at the dainty watch on her wrist. "Afraid not Rose, honey. I'm supposed to meet those two crooks in front of Happy's bar in ten minutes. I gotta beat it."

"I know."

She pulled away slowly from Glenda's arms. She walked to the chair, pushed up the red rain coat and held it up for Glenda, who slipped into it quickly and belted it securely.

"Well?" inquired Glenda.

Rose surveyed the beautiful creature appraisingly. "Perfect." She then handed her a pair of dark glasses.

"Don't you think the dark glasses are a little out of place in the rain?"

"It's either that or the possibility of being recognized if they get too close. "

Glenda put on the glasses, then turned to the door and opened it. Rose ran quickly to her. A quick peck on the lips, then, "Be careful Glenda darling."

"I will . . . See you soon!"

Rose closed the door and leaned tearfully against it listening to Glenda's high heels click on the wooden stairs in the hall just beyond.

CHAPTER TWENTY-EIGHT

Before Glenda ventured out onto the street she pulled the coat collar up as far as it would go around her neck. Calmly then, without looking around but knowing the watchful eye of Mac and Ernie were on her, she moved to her car, got in and drove off.

"We're gonna roust that bitch right after we pick up the cash. She's gettin' around too much. I ain't lookin' to catch some bug from her," said Mac.

"Yeah. I'd say Rosie ain't no good for us no more," added Ernie. "We'll get one of the boys to proposition her then move in for the kill."

Mac laughed. "Old Hazel out at the farm sure will love us for that. Maybe she's got somethin' out there to trade."

Mac laughed harder as Ernie joined in. "You bet your sweet ever lovin'." Then the laugh died in his throat. "Get going." He spat his words out quickly.

"What?"

"I said get this car moving fast. Scream that siren."

"Where to?"

"After his car."

Mac jammed the gears home. The wheels spun on the wet ground, then took hold. The car shot forward. "What's up?" Mac was still puzzled.

"Where would Rosie get enough ready cash to buy a car like that?"

"Holy Christ—You're right." Mac pressed his foot harder on the accelerator. "That's him in Rosie's red get up."

"You're gettin' real smart. Shut up and concentrate on driving."

"I can cut him off up the line by radio."

"You nuts or somethin'? That guy's gotta be dead before any other cop gets to him."

"Yeah—Yeah—Guess I wasn't thinkin'." Mac skidded the car around a corner. The wheels slid across the wet pavement then shot forward again after creasing a parked car fender.

"I told you to blast that siren," shouted Ernie.

Mac put the siren into action. Both had always enjoyed the thrill of the chase but there was a deeper meaning this time. Their own lives could be at stake. Neither one of them had the slightest desire to hear the cell doors clang shut from the wrong side.

Mac nervously looked down to the speedometer, then his eyes snapped up to the road again as a pedestrian jumped out of the way just in the nick of time.

"Keep your eyes on the road damn it," shouted Ernie.

"I am—I am."

"These cow jerks get in the way run 'em over."

"I might just hafta do that little thing. Say we oughta be seein' him by now!"

"He had a good head start."

"Maybe he turned off. "

"Where? He was headin' this way and there

ain't no turn offs and he sure didn't come back toward us. Don't kid yourself. He's hittin' it this way and fast. We gotta get him before some of the other state boys hit him for speeding."

"If they do we sure'll catch hell for not radio'n ahead."

"If they do we catch hell for more'n that, Mac." Ernie strained his eyes ahead along the road. "There he is, up there 'bout half a mile."

Glenda had heard the distant siren. Through her rear view mirror she saw the police car behind and moving in fast. Their car was sure to have more speed than hers. Her only chance was to hit it off the main highway, take the cliff road out over the fair grounds. Possibly the steep mountainous roads could give her more time.

She spun the wheel, cutting off onto the lesser road.

"He's heading out the fair ground road," shouted Ernie.

"We got him now. He can't make no time on that crazy mountain road."

"Neither can we."

"We better—if you know what's good for us."

The police car reached the cut off and without slacking speed Mac spun the car, on two wheels and in a cloud of mud and dirty rain water, off the main highway. In so doing the front fender caught the edge of the fair grounds sign, sending the sign flying into a hundred splinters.

"You tryin' to get us killed?"

"I always did say that sign was too close to the

road. Throw a couple of shots at him—Maybe we'll get lucky."

"We'll be close enough for just that in a minute." Ernie lowered the window with one hand while he unholstered his gun with the other.

"Get his tire."

"Tire hell—That's too small a target. I'm gonna try for him—right in the back of the head. That red hat makes a fair target." He fired.

The bullet crashed through Glenda's rear window and shattered the windshield just to her right. The second bullet hit within an inch of the first. Glenda ducked low over the steering wheel at the same time pushing her accelerator to the floor.

"He went around that bend up ahead. I'll get him the next shot." Ernie leveled his pistol—preparing.

Then both froze in their seats. One of the big carnival trucks came around the bend fast. Both the driver of the truck and Mac spun their wheels—but both in the wrong direction. They hit head on and in a grinding, crashing sound of glass and twisting steel the vehicles, cemented to each other, hit through the guard railing to go end over end down the face of the cliff.

* * * *

Rose was glad the rain had stopped. Although she really did like the rain she didn't relish driving in it even with an experienced driver such as the bus driver she knew to be an expert.

She pulled her red camel hair coat tightly around her middle, checked her baggage with the attendant, bought a newspaper then sat down to wait her scheduled time of departure.

Mac and Ernie's pictures on the front page caught her immediate attention even before the big black headlines which told her: "POLICE OFFICERS KILLED IN CRASH." A light smile of appreciation crossed her lips.

Rose's bus was announced over the loud speaker. She got up, dropped the newspaper and moved to the bus ramp.

CHAPTER TWENTY-NINE

The Mouse sat at the same back corner table in the Spot Seventeen. Jake, while polishing some of the grime from his thick beer glasses, kept his eye on the little creep. The last time, when the "cute little chick" in the fuzzy sweater had tossed a Martini in the creep's face Jake had tossed him out on his ear and among his curses told him to "stay out" in no uncertain terms. But here he was again—and at the same table too. When he had first come in Jake had the instant urge to toss him out even harder than the last time, but he seemed to be staying straight enough—besides—maybe that pretty thing would meet him like the last time. Even the thought stirred him deep inside.

"Damn—if she comes in this time I'm sure gonna find out her name. Wonder if she'd go for a guy like me?"

Thus engrossed, Jake in his silent words, turned to view himself in the mirror. "Ah—too damned fat. Maybe if I shave." Pause. "What the hell can a shave do for a kisser like mine. Kisser? Huh! It ain't been even kissed in five years. That old battle ax of mine—Huh! Who needs that fat slob anyway." A vision of he and his wife in bed crossed his mind's eye and all he could think about were elephants.

He turned quickly from the mirror as the door opened.

The girl who entered was too tall—too lean— overly made up and her bright red hair looked more like a wig than hair. The tight jersey dress underneath her light coat proved the lady to be almost shapeless—except for the oversized breasts—undoubtedly phony.

Jake watched the long nylon clad legs carry her across to sit beside the Mouse. "Christ—she looks like one of them village drags—Maybe he—she is—What the hell."

"Bring her a beer!" Mouse was his demanding self that Jake remembered.

Jake would take little of that stuff. He poured the beer and took it to the table.

To the Mouse: "You want another?"

"If I did I'd a told you so."

Jake was going to get damned mad—damned soon. "Ah what the hell. His money is as good as anybody's." He spun away and walked back to the bar. "That broad still looks like some guy dressed up like a broad."

Jake only shook his head at the thought.

Mouse pointed to the beer. "I buy the first one—and no more."

"Thanks." The voice matched the frame. Coarse. Hard. It could never pass for female.

Even Mouse was amazed. "You'll last about one job."

"I've been at it three years."

"It don't figger." He slugged down the remainder of his drink. "What are you called?"

"Pauline."

"The boy name."

"Paul."

163

"That figgers . . . Sure don't figger the syndicate pickin' one like you."

"Look buster . . ."

"No—You look—I don't like drags. I ain't never liked drags and I ain't never gonna like drags. I'm a middle man. I just pass on the orders and you carry them out. Understand?"

"So order."

"You got a long plane trip ahead."

"I like planes." She drank. "Where?"

"Los Angeles."

"Who do I do the job on?"

"One of your own kind, doll—one of your own kind."

THE END

164